BABY DADDY RESCUE

A HOT SINGLE DAD ROMANCE #2

ANGEL DEVLIN

TRACY LORRAINE

Editing by Andie M. Long

Cover design and formatting by Dandelion Cover Designs

A NOTE

Baby Daddy Rescue is written in British English and contains British spelling and grammar. This may appear incorrect to some readers when compared to US English books.

Angel & Tracy xo

1

KAYLIE

AS I BURST in through the door, the other ladies in the bathroom all turn to look at me. Sympathy flashes across a few faces. That means they've either seen, or worse, smelled my date.

I'm burned by almost every date arranged online, yet my desperation to find the one still keeps me returning to my laptop or phone.

Dropping down onto the closed toilet seat, I suck in some clean, albeit bathroom air, and pull my phone from my bag. It's been vibrating on my lap for the last few minutes as if even my phone knows this is my most disastrous date out of all the horrendous ones that have gone before.

I almost sigh when I see my best friend's name

appear on my screen. He seems to always know just when I need him.

Aiden: How's it going?

Me: Fucking disaster. I'm surprised you can't smell him from wherever you are.

I add the little throwing up emoji and hit send, expecting a handful of laughing gifs back.

Aiden: Want me to come rescue you?

My heart swells knowing that he'd ditch whatever he's doing tonight—probably some unsuspecting female who's about to get fucked and chucked faster than she can blink.

Me: No, it's fine. I've got this.

What I need is a knight in shining fucking armour to sweep me away and do all sorts of wicked things to me. I don't need to force Aiden away from adding another notch on his bedpost.

I take my time washing my hands and spray a

little extra perfume across my body, hoping that it might cover up my date's putrid stench.

Plastering a smile on my face, I head back out. He might be all kinds of wrong for me, but I'm also not a heartless bitch and I couldn't walk out the moment I arrived. I just don't have it in me. All I can hope now is that he pays for the meal so at least I can say I had some free food, even if it was all tainted by his smell.

"There you are. I thought maybe you'd fallen in."
Sadly not.

"Sorry, there was a queue." Mark glances around the half-empty restaurant but he says nothing.

"I hope you don't mind but I've ordered our desserts."

"Oh... uh..."

"Apple pie all around. It's been too long since Mummy made it for me."

Raising an eyebrow, I don't ask because he's already explained more than once in our hour of being here about how he still lives with his mother and has no intentions of moving out any time soon while she still does everything for him. *Shame she doesn't make him shower.*

"I don't actually like—"

My words are cut off when two bowls are placed in front of us.

"Enjoy." The waiter is different to the others we've had all night and as I look up, I can see why. The others are all huddled in the corner laughing. I'm glad my Friday night misery is entertaining them. And I haven't even got the melt-in-the-middle chocolate pudding I spied when ordering. I bloody love chocolate. I hate apples.

"Mmm... so good," Mark mumbles, little bits of pie flying from his mouth, making me want to puke in mine.

I pick at the vanilla ice cream that's sitting on the side but mostly I just watch it melt. That is until a very familiar voice fills my ears and has my spine straightening.

"What the hell do you think you're doing?"

Running my eyes up Aiden's tall and lean body, I can't help but note every difference to the man sitting opposite me.

"I'm sorry, do you mind? I'm on a date."

"Yeah with my girlfriend. Care to explain why?" Aiden leans in. I see the exact moment he regrets it because his cheeks puff out as if he's gagging.

"I'm... I'm sorry... She was on..."

"I don't care." Turning his amused, although slightly repulsed eyes to me, he can't help but notice the almost full bowl sitting in front of me. "Come on, baby. Let's get you home. You're in for a spanking tonight."

Mark splutters before Aiden's giant hand wraps around my upper arm and I'm pulled so I'm standing right in front of him.

"And you wore my favourite dress. You know what that thing does to me." He growls, actually fucking growls like a wild animal as he puts on a great show of checking me out.

Chancing a glance at Mark, I note he looks like he's about to shit his pants any minute. Although from the smell permeating the air, we could argue that he already has.

"Come on, sweet cheeks," I let out a surprised squeal as Aiden's hand lands on my arse. "Let's get you home. I've been dying to—" He drops his lips to my ear as if he's whispering something filthy but instead he says. "Fuck me, he smells so bad. How did you sit there so long?"

I'm full on belly laughing as together we make our way out of the restaurant doors and into the night.

"If you insist on keeping up with shitty online

dating, then you need to start being a little more selective."

"You think I'd have chosen him if he'd looked like that in his profile picture? Shit, I know I'm bordering on desperate, but fuck, Aid."

"Come on, let's go and get you drunk."

His fingers intertwine with mine and he pulls me in the direction of a bar around the corner.

We find a couple of seats right in the window of Brewdog's and sit down with our beers watching the world go past outside.

"You don't need to babysit me for the rest of the night. Feel free to go back to whatever woman you were trying to pull."

"Nah, you're okay. It was kinda slim pickings tonight."

"Really?" I pop an eyebrow at him. Aiden Thomson never has issues picking up women no matter how bad a night it might be.

"Yeah. I just wasn't really into it tonight."

"Uh... who are you and what have you done with my best friend? If you start trying to tell me you're done with all that and want to think about settling down, then Hell really has frozen over."

"Would it be so hard to believe?" He places a

hand to his chest and affects a 'hurt feelings' expression.

"Yeah, it really would. Have you met someone?" I ask with interest. In all the years I've known Aiden, he's never had more than two dates with a woman. It's obviously going to happen someday, and part of me can't wait for someone special to capture his heart, but another part loves that he rides the 'forever single' train with me. Everyone else in my life is getting their shit together but my shit keeps slipping through my fingers... *uh what a shit analogy.*

"What's wrong?" Aiden asks taking a long pull on his beer.

"I just feel like I'm being left behind. I'm thirty next week and I've got none of the things I always said I wanted."

"Does it matter?"

"Yes, it matters." I stroke condensation from the side of my glass. "I'm getting older and with every passing year I'm just one step closer to not having the family I want."

From as early as I can remember all I've wanted is to be a mum. While other girls in school would dream of being doctors and astronauts, teachers would look at me with slight horror when I said I just wanted to be a mum. I can't help it, something within me just needs it.

"It'll happen, Kay."

"That's what everyone keeps telling me, but I'm fed up of fucking waiting. I'm starting to think maybe I should take matters into my own hands." Now that gets his full attention.

"How exactly?" he asks hesitantly. "I'm sure your date would be more than willing, although he probably wouldn't have a clue where he should be sticking what." I think back to the poor guy we left sitting with his apple pie and laugh. I'm sure he's lovely really and his perfect woman is also out there somewhere; someone lacking a sense of smell.

"I think I need to update my profile. Make myself look a little more desirable, you know what I mean?"

"You're beautiful just as you are."

"While it's great that you think that, I keep getting matched with idiots. I need someone who gets me, who understands what I want. Is that so hard to find?"

"You're asking the wrong guy."

I let out a sigh as a happy couple walk in front of us. His arm is around her shoulders and she's looking up at him with such love and adoration it actually makes my heart hurt.

"Will you help me?"

"Me? How?"

"You get matched with someone about every ten minutes. I bet you've had a gazillion while we've been sitting here, and I'd put money on the fact some of them are in this exact bar. Show me how you do it. Teach me what I need to find the right guy."

"Kaylie," he lets out an exasperated breath. "I might get plenty of matches but I'm offering up something very different to what you're looking for. Girls don't come to me looking for forever, thank fuck. They just want a good time."

"To be honest, I'd settle for that right now. It's been sooo long."

"Stop, I can't listen to this. It's like talking to my sister about sex."

"Oh, so you can quite happily brag about what you've been up to, but I can't even mention my never-ending dry spell?"

"Exactly. I'm glad you understand."

Groaning in frustration, my head falls onto my arms on the table in front of me. Everyone around me is in the middle of experiencing their happily ever afters and here I am going backwards. At least if

I were shagging about a bit I might have some fun instead of just a string of bad dates.

Aiden pulls his phone out and as predicted, he's got a mile long list of notifications. I don't blame any of the women who want him. He's gorgeous, charismatic; the sweetest guy I've ever met. If only he wanted something serious, he could be the perfect guy. I laugh at my thoughts, the beer's clearly going to my head if I'm thinking these kinds of things.

"I think I need to go home." The hiccup that follows is just proof I'm making the right decision. The bottle of wine I had at the restaurant to drown my sorrows was enough. I didn't really need to add the beer on top.

"Come on, I'll walk you."

"No, no. I'll just get a taxi. You go and enjoy the rest of your night."

He gives me a look that stops any further arguments. He's always been overprotective of me and it seems right now is no different.

"Don't worry, I'm not going to go and booty call my date."

"I should fucking hope not. I can still smell him. Can you imagine how bad he tastes? Ouch," Aiden complains when I slap his shoulder.

"I think I was just sick in my mouth."

Our walk back to my place is mostly in silence. I'm too busy stewing on the disaster my life has turned out to be. I can only imagine that Aiden is mourning the girls he could be touching up on the dance floor right now instead of walking me home like a good little boy.

"Where's Cheryl?" he asks when we walk into a dark flat.

"Out with Rick."

"Is it getting serious then?"

"Yeah, very, by the looks of it. She's never here. If it weren't for the fact she still pays half the rent, I'd think she'd moved in with him. It's coming though and I've no idea what I'm going to do. I can't afford this place on my own and the thought of trying to find a new roommate... ugh... it'll be just like dating, only worse because I'll have to live with them."

"It'll all work itself out, Kay. You'll see."

"How can you be so positive all the time?"

"One of my many charms." Shrugging off his coat, he falls down onto my sofa and slips his shoes off. "You got any beer?"

Sometimes I wish I was more like my best friend. Nothing seems to bother him at all.

2

AIDEN

OKAY, let's get all this stuff out of the way first.

I'm a firefighter.

Yes, I have a huge hose. Yes, lots of women like to swing on my pole. And taking my name in vain, I'm always coming to women's 'Aid'—as they scream it in orgasm usually.

Kaylie is my best friend. I've known her since school and she's been a lovable disaster since she was six and accidentally knocked a pot of paint-mixed-with-water all over my favourite Thomas the Tank Engine t-shirt. But she said sorry by giving me her morning bottle of milk and we've been friends ever since.

Now the milk's changed to beer but everything else is pretty much the same.

Another date for Kaylie. Another rescue by Aiden.

She passes me my beer and sits beside me on the sofa.

"I don't know how you manage it, babes. Seriously." I take a swig of my beer.

"Well dating apps don't come with an optional 'smell your date' facility, do they?" she answers haughtily.

I fart. Can't help it, it's the position I'm sitting in.

She wafts dramatically. "Oh for fuck's sake, Aiden."

"Improvement on what you've been smelling all night."

"Even though that's the truth you are not forgiven for tainting my nostrils when they were just enjoying a reprieve."

My phone beeps. Cassie wanting to know if I want a repeat.

I text her a 'no thanks, I've got a new girlfriend', block her number and delete the contact.

"Let me guess. Another woman wanting a booty call?"

"I can't help it if they find my body and the whole firefighter rescue thing hot as fuck. I'm paid to dampen down the heat. It's an extra service I provide."

"You're such a slut."

"You're just jealous cos you're not getting any."

"I knowwwww." She throws herself backwards dramatically on the sofa. "I need a man. I need sex. I want a family."

"And what's that noise? Elephant stampede? No, just every guy in the vicinity running away from the needy woman in apartment 12A."

She sits back up. "It's not fair, Aiden. I went to see Jenson, Leah, and Amelia last night. They're so excited about the new baby. They're the perfect little family and now Auntie Kaylie just isn't needed as much anymore."

I see her bottom lip wobble. Still reminds me of when she was six and thought I was going to push her for spilling water on me. I shuffle closer and wrap my arms around her.

"Kay. They're in the honeymoon phase. Give it a bit of time when that newborn is screeching and Amelia's having a major tantrum and your phone will be ringing while they beg for a rare night out."

"I guess so, but I want my own family, Aid. Maybe I'll have to go look at men who provide your kind of services."

I feel my body tense. "No! Not unless there are no other options, Kay, and at the moment there are other options."

The other service I provided? I was a sperm donor.

That's right. I donated sperm to a bank where over the course of my lifetime I can end up with children in up to ten families that aren't mine. Every one of those children will have the right to know who fathered them and my last known address when they reach eighteen years of age, and that's fine with me because I'll tell them my reasons no problem.

My twin sister had to use a sperm donation to achieve her family after years of struggling to conceive. And we're close, me and Steph. Her journey to motherhood was fraught and I shared some of that pain. If I can do anything to help another woman like someone helped my sister, then that's my total pleasure... in a vial.

I'm such a goddamn hero, right?

Hell, I hope I'm not coming across as too much of a tosser, although of course I am. I donate to a sperm bank remember? I love my family, we're all very close, and especially me and Steph and my two nephews, Adam and Thomas, who are now four.

"I'm almost thirty." Kay's whining brings me out of my head. "I feel like time's running out."

"Well, it's not. You still have time to find the man of your dreams and do things the way you always wanted. And don't tell me you didn't keep that piece of paper you wrote when you were fifteen about your ideal wedding because I know you. That shit is imprinted in your brain."

"Yeah, well reality is making me think twice about all my romantic notions. And if I want more than one kid, then maybe I do need to consider the route of artificial insemination." She looks at my face which no doubt is telling her I'm getting pissed off. I can feel my hackles rising.

"I'm not saying I'm definitely doing it. Just that I can't rule it out anymore. It's an option. I just wish you could pay a donor to come do it the natural way with romance and candlelight rather than how you describe it."

"See. You need to find love and your family via the romantic way."

She sighed. "Can't you get someone to do it the hearts and flowers way?"

"Oh yeah." I take my arm away from behind her neck and stand up, ready now to start ranting. "You can get some dickhead off the internet who's not screened and they can come round and shag you the old fashioned way. Not likely to be romantic though is it if they turn up like tonight's date and you have to put a peg on your nose so you can open your legs long enough for them to make their deposit, and then they know where you live and can come claim their parental rights and you have to see Smelly Daddy midweek and every other weekend to pass your kid over."

"Okay, okay. I have time to do it the proper way. I'd better up my dating game instead to give me more of a chance."

I sigh; a long, drawn-out sigh. "I'd better clear my calendar then, so I can come rescue you even more often."

She looks up at me and grins. "I know I'm a pain in your arse, but you love me, and you're stuck with me."

I flop back down onto the sofa at the side of her.

"Yes, I do, and I will always come rescue you. I'll just bring some Lynx next time to spray your date with."

I fart again.

"That's it." Kay jumps up and I watch her baggy clothes flopping around her as she waves her hand in the direction of the door. "Out. Go home now,

Aiden. You're a smelly boy. I need freedom from smelly boys."

I finish my beer and kiss her cheek as I head for the door.

"Love ya, Kay-bear. Don't give up. Your knight in fragranced armour is out there somewhere."

"Love ya, too. Now fuck off before you fart again."

She closes the door on me and I laugh as I do indeed let one rip as I walk away.

MY WATCH ARE in the mess room the next morning when the alarm rings and we spring into action.

"Office on Silver Street, AFA activated." Jasper, our gaffer reads out.

Chances are it's just a routine call when the AFA —the automatic fire alarm—goes off, but you can't take that for granted. We attend every situation like it could be life or death, because sometimes it is. We see things in this job that can take you a long time to accept, things no one should ever see. If you sat with us in the mess room when we bantered black humour around the place you'd probably think we were wankers, but it's how you learn to deal with the horror you see from the worst situations. My watch are family. We have to be. We share experiences and keep each other safe.

Sure enough the AFA has been set off by a toaster and once I've done the checks we're ready to leave. But not before I've flirted with a few of the female office staff. Even the older guys on the crew with their bald heads and beer bellies are elevated to Sex God status when they dress in the firefighter uniform. It does sometimes piss me off that the women act like a male stripper just walked in, rather than someone trying to make sure they don't burn to death, but it's par for the course and sometimes I trade on that same firefighter appeal to get laid, so I can't be too much of a hypocrite.

"Thanks for coming. I'm so sorry. I went to answer the phone and didn't realise the crumpet got stuck in the toaster." The blonde flicks her fringe out of her face and smiles at me like she's Marilyn Monroe reincarnated. "I'll have to be careful not to do it again." She simpers. "Unless... you'd like to see me again?"

I stand up straight and look down at her, my face tense. "The callout to your burned crumpet cost the fire service in the region of two grand in running costs and man hours."

Her face drains of colour.

"So, maybe next time you could be a bit more careful, hey? It can also potentially take us away from a major incident."

"I'm sorry. I didn't realise." I think blondie's about to cry. Fuck.

"No worries. We get tons of calls for toasters. Just concentrate on you being the hot stuff hey?" I quip as I wink and leave the building.

THE REST of the day passes without major incident and by six pm I'm eating my way through a packet of crumpets (the blonde made me hungry but not for her). I've not heard anything from Kay but given she's a primary school teacher she'll have been dealing with snotty noses and budding future friendships all day. I often wonder if it's our friendship that put her on that career path, but I've never got up the guts to actually ask her in case she laughed in my face and said I was soppy. That wouldn't do for my alpha arsehole image at all.

I send her a Snapchat of my face with a tiger head filter.

Hot stuff: (yep that's my username, deal with it). **How's your day been? Any dates tonight you'll need potentially rescuing from?**

I see her open it and I get a message back.

KaylieH: Nope, you're safe. The lovebirds are out so making the most of the peace and quiet. Probably cry into my supper later.

Hot stuff: You're supposed to send a photo back with text, not just text. Do you know anything about the modern world at all?

KaylieH: photo of her holding her middle finger up at the screen. **I'm a dinosaur. That's my whole problem. I'm gonna go extinct before I find love.**

Hot stuff: Holding up a Chinese takeaway leaflet. **Get your arse around here. Let's go**

through Tinder and also I want to check your dating profiles. Let's get you a man. One who washes himself.

KaylieH: Photo with a big smiling face. **Chinese! My favourite. On my way.**

I laugh at her saying it's her favourite food. I think I might know that given I've known the girl for twenty-four years.

It's time to give her some lessons in love and the ways of a hot-blooded male. Time for your fire training Miss Hale. Let's get some male libidos burning for you.

3

KAYLIE

I KNOCK on Aiden's front door but it's only out of courtesy as I then push the solid door open and let myself inside. It's not happened yet but I know that one day I'm going to come walking in and find him in a compromising position.

I know he spends most of his free time either in the gym or in a woman and the latter is really something I don't want to witness.

"In the kitchen," he calls.

When I round the corner, I find tubs of takeaway food on the counter along with a large glass of wine waiting for me. I can't help but think it looks like I've just barged in on him waiting for his date. Not that he dates. There's even a fucking candle burning on the windowsill.

"Um... are you expecting company?"

"Yeah, and she's just arrived."

"This is for me?"

"It's just a takeaway, Kay. It's not like I opened the oven or anything."

"Fair enough." Slipping my coat off, I drop it over the back of a chair and reach out for the wine. I've had the day from hell, so this is most definitely welcome.

"Glad to see you dressed up for the occasion."

"What?" I look down at my oversized jumper dress and leggings and shrug. "It's cute."

"Is it?"

"As if you know anything about fashion."

"I don't claim to know anything. But what I do know is what turns a guy on and I can say without a doubt that a dress like that, that hides every single thing underneath, isn't it."

"Whatever," I say, waving him off and taking a sip of my wine. "Oh, that's good."

"I should hope so, it's your favourite."

"What did I do to deserve this?"

"Just thought you needed cheering up. Plus, if we're going to sex up your profile, I thought you might need some alcohol in your system."

My forehead creases. "What exactly does 'sexing

up my profile' mean? I'm not exposing myself for the whole world to see."

"As much as that would be a sure fire way to get a guy's interest, it's not what I was suggesting."

"So what are you suggesting?"

"Let's eat... and drink. Then we'll have a look and see what we can do."

———

"WHERE THE HELL do you put all that?" I ask Aiden when he's cleared his plate of his original serving and his seconds.

"A machine this well-tuned needs good fuel, Kay-bear."

"Please don't use that name. You know I hate it."

"Aw, but it's so cute."

"Yeah... just like my dress."

He snorts, just about managing to keep the swig of beer he just had in his mouth.

"I've left my laptop in the living room. Go and log into your dating profile of choice and I'll just clean this lot up and join you."

Grabbing my wine, I get the hell out of the kitchen before he convinces me to help him. He's got a way of making women do exactly as he wants, and sadly at times I'm not immune to his charms.

Resting back on his sofa with his laptop on my knees, I log in and go straight for my new matches. I've got two. One is a bald guy who looks to be at least fifty, although his profile states that he's actually thirty-five.

"Nice fucking try, mate," I mutter, taking another sip of wine, hoping it might make the next guy look a little better.

Clicking to the next one, my eyes widen slightly. He looks normal, which immediately makes me suspicious. He must be hiding something. Scanning through his information, nothing stands out to me as weird. Maybe I've found the one normal guy on this site.

Name: Tate Wright

Age: 32

Occupation: Librarian

"Li-fucking-brarian. Next," Aiden says from his position looking over my shoulder.

"Fucking hell, judgemental much?"

"Oh come off it. He'll be a right boring fuck."

"Do you mean that figuratively or literally?"

"Uh... both."

"He might spend his days reading romance novels to discover what women really want."

"Oh yeah, because that'll make him an expert on women."

"Like you?"

"Yeah, like me."

"Well, that's it. My other match was an old guy claiming to be in his thirties. So other than this guy, I'm out of options."

"That's what I'm about to fix. Shift."

I lift my legs and allow him to sit on his own sofa, before dropping them back to rest on his legs, leaving him nowhere to place the laptop. Groaning, he turns to balance it on the armrest.

"Jesus, Kay, could you sound anymore dull and desperate?"

"What? I was just trying to be honest."

"Primary school teacher who loves kids and can't wait to have a family of my own," he mocks in a voice that I assume is meant to sound like me. "Only equally desperate douchebags are going to respond to this. No man wants to date a woman whose only interest is having a family."

"But guys want kids too," I argue.

"Yeah, but they also want to have some fun before the serious shit happens. So sell them the fun, show them what you've got to offer." he makes a boobs gesture with his hands.

"I'm not showing them my tits, Aid."

"I wasn't suggesting you did, not yet anyway. Just tease. Show them you've got something worth meeting in person."

"Jesus, you make it sound like I need to be some kind of stripper to get a decent date."

"Hey now, I never made any promises about decent. Just hopefully sweeter smelling than the last one."

I groan as memories from that disastrous night fill my mind. "I just want a good guy," I fake cry and drop my head into the cushion.

"We'll find you one, babes. Now plaster a smile on your face, we're replacing all of these dull ass photos of yourself looking like the unsexiest woman on the planet."

"I'm unsexy? Well, this night really is looking up."

"No, of course not. Well, I don't think so. You're always hiding in these godawful clothes so I'm not really sure what's beneath. You could be covered in scales as far as I know."

"You've seen me in a swimming costume." I

frown at him, more pissed off about what he thinks than I should be.

"We were seven. A lot changes between then and adulthood."

Rolling my eyes at him, I pull my legs off his in a huff.

"What are you waiting for?"

"What?" I snap. This whole thing was a stupid idea. I should just continue dating idiots and hope Mr Right suddenly appears, then die miserable and alone when he doesn't show his face.

"Get up and get that fucking awful dress off."

"No fucking chance am I getting naked in front of you."

"Did I say anything about getting naked? No, I didn't. You're wearing something underneath it, right?"

"Yeah, but—" My words are cut off when he stands, reaches behind his head and pulls his t-shirt over his head.

My chin drops at the inches of toned and tanned skin he reveals.

"Careful, you'll start drooling any moment."

"Fuck off, it was just shock."

"Suuuure it was. Your turn."

"What, are we six? I'll show you mine if you show me yours?"

"I hadn't considered that but if you're up for it then..." his hands drop to his waistband.

"No, no, no," I say in a panic. I haven't seen a naked man in... a very long time and I don't intend on my next one being my best friend.

Gripping the bottom of my dress, I pull it up and over my head then drop it to the floor. My arms automatically wrap around my middle in an attempt to hide my belly that I hate even though it's covered in a vest.

"See, that's the problem."

My eyes almost pop out of my head that Aiden's about to tell me I look horrible. That's not the kind of help I came here for tonight.

"Your lack of confidence. It's a turn off. You need to be proud of who you are and what you've got."

Walking over, he places his hands on my shoulders and pushes them back.

"Stand up straight. It'll make you look more confident, plus it'll..." he looks down at my breasts and his voice catches. "Um... it'll make your tits look better. See, look in the mirror." He points to the one hanging over the fireplace.

"Okay, so to attract a man I've got to walk about with my tits out. What else, oh wise one?"

He's not really telling me anything I don't know. I know my confidence has taken a huge knock. That came courtesy of my one and only long-term relationship. The day he left he seemed to take all of my self-esteem with him.

"Hair. You've got gorgeous thick hair." Turning me, he pulls the band out that's holding the mass of curls at the base of my neck and runs his fingers through it to give it some volume. "See, so much better and I haven't really done anything. Now let's get some pictures of you looking sexy and confident."

He pulls his phone from his pocket and holds it up to me. My shoulders instantly slump again. "I hate having my photo taken."

"I know. But it's just you and me messing around. Forget about the real reason." He takes a few but without looking at them I know the smile on my face is fake. "You remember that night we went camping with my parents?"

"The night you told me ghost stories that haunted me for weeks to come? Yeah, I remember that pretty well. It's one of the reasons I still can't watch horror movies."

"That was a good weekend."

"It really was." Aiden continues bringing up fun times from the past and together we laugh at the memories and the stupid shit we did as kids. Before I know it, I've drained my second glass of wine and I'm feeling pretty good.

"I think we're done."

"Done?" I've totally forgotten about the camera in his hands and the fact we're both half dressed.

"Yeah, look." He goes to step around the coffee table with his phone stretched out for me to see but after one too many beers, his foot gets caught on the corner and he comes flying towards me. My back hits the wall and he just about manages to catch himself by placing his hands either side of my head.

"Fuck." Standing to full height, his deep blue eyes stare down into mine; his heaving, naked chest just noticeable. I've no idea if he does it on purpose but he closes the space between us, his chest brushing mine causing electric sparks to shoot off around my body.

Jesus, it's been too long since I got laid.

"Aiden, what are you doing? You're drunk."

"Oh right, yeah. My head's feeling pretty fuzzy right about now."

"I think I'd better call a cab."

"Yeah, erm, okay," he mutters, standing back and

allowing me space to grab my dress from the floor and pull it back on.

"Thanks for tonight."

"If you leave your account logged in, I'll upload the best of the photos for you. I'm sure you'll be overwhelmed with matches."

"That would be awesome." Once I've collected my coat and bag, I walk back up to where he's still standing in the exact same spot. "I'll call you tomorrow." Reaching up on my tiptoes, I kiss his rough cheek, thank him again and head for home feeling a little more confident about my dating future than when I arrived.

4

AIDEN

NO.

NO. NO. NO. NO. NO.

How do I get my mind to empty?

I might have to employ a hypnotherapist.

Visions of my best friend in her tight vest top, the swell of her breasts poking out at the top won't leave my mind.

GET OUT.

I'm not doing this.

SHE'S. MY. BEST. FRIEND.

WE. DON'T. THINK. OF. HER. THAT. WAY.

Weeee doooo nowwww. My brain fights back.

I throw myself on the sofa. The ceiling tilts a bit with the amount of beer I've consumed this evening.

Put it down to the booze, mate. In the morning she'll be back in your brain as the best friend who walks around looking like she's homeless or eighty-four years old. It'll be fine.

I close my eyes and let the alcohol send me into oblivion.

Kaylie is standing in the doorway to my bedroom in her vest top and itty-bitty red lace panties. Her index finger is pulling on the bottom of her lip.

"Hey, Kay-bear. What are you doing here?"

She pulls the vest top up and over her head, revealing creamy titties with rosebud-pink puckered nipples.

"I want you to fuck me, Aid. I'm, well, I never told you this, but I'm a virgin."

My cock almost punches out of the duvet in response. I watch as she drops her panties, kicking them away and then she walks over to the bed.

I pull the duvet back to reveal my six-pack and my rock-hard length.

"I need you sooo baddd, Aiden. Let me..."

She sits astride me and despite her 'virgin' status, her hand grips my length and she guides me inside her. She's warm and so wet, her juices soaking me and I sink into her depths. She lifts up and down, circling

*around and gaining a steady rhythm, licking around
her lips as she does it.*
"Fuck, Aiden, Fuck."

I WAKE up on the sofa to find I've got my cock in
my hand and drool running from the corner of my
mouth. Fuck the drool. I pump my cock carrying on
the fantasy in my brain, imagining Kaylie is riding
my cock until I come in my fist.

And then I want to die with shame because
that's my first ever sex-dream about my best friend. I
have never, ever seen her that way, at ALL, until last
night when I saw a glimpse of her tits.

I go clean up while I berate myself. I'm pathetic.
A totally pathetic paid-up member of the male
species and I should be flogged for my crimes. But
something's nagging at me and I hate the fact the
dream seemed so real.

Kaylie will be up now. I dial her number.

"Kay-bear?"

"Bit fucking early for you this, isn't it? You shit
the bed?"

"Daft question but... you're not a virgin are you?"

There's a long awkward silence before she snaps.

"Of course I'm not a fucking virgin. I dated Phillip for years for a start. Plus, I've told you about when I lost it and how awkward it all was."

"I just wanted to check you weren't lying."

"Why? Would I get more hits on the dating site if I said I was? Actually don't answer that. I can work that answer out for myself. Are you still pissed? Have you not actually gone to bed, just carried on drinking?"

"I'm just updating your profile." I lied, "and yeah, you're right, stupid question, stupid idea."

"Certifiable you are sometimes, Aiden Thomson. Now go away, I have more intelligent people to hang around with today, and they're all five so that's saying something."

She hangs up and I groan again.

I really do need to make her dating profile.

First, a shower and breakfast.

I'm not working today and once I've done this profile I'm off to visit my sister and the kids. I sit down with a slice of toast and fire up the laptop that had run out of juice and switched itself off while I was in my beer coma. I upload the photos from my phone. The photos of Kaylie begin to flash up on the screen as thumbnails. Wow, I took a LOT. Thirty-six photos in fact. Clicking onto the first one I bring it up close.

On this one Kaylie is still standing like she has a crooked wire coat hanger down her back. Awkward and ungainly. Her untied hair hangs in her face. I feel a stab of affection for my awkward but lovely best friend. As I click along the snaps, the pictures become something else entirely as Kaylie sheds her awkwardness with each subsequent shot. She's laughing, the wine having loosened her up. Her eyes are sparkling, whether through laughter or alcohol it reveals more of her joviality. She's fluffed and rearranged her hair and it cascades over her shoulders and I want to reach in and run my hands through it.

What?

I shove the laptop away from me like it's a contagious disease.

I will tell myself one more time, I say in my head sharply. BEST FRIEND RIGHT THERE. OKAY?

My dick hardens in response.

Stupid dumbass male body.

Regardless of the fact my mind and body are betraying me right now, I have a task to do; so like the hero I am, I crop the photos, making them the best they can be. I don't doctor them in any way; to be honest she doesn't need it.

Opening her dating profile, I add a headshot and a full-length and then I start to edit her profile.

Name: Kaylie Hale

Occupation: ~~Primary School Teacher.~~ Full time temptress.

Age: ~~29.~~ Old enough ;)

Looking for: ~~Primary school teacher who loves kids and can't wait to have a family of my own.~~ Hot single man to treat me like a goddess.

I CARRY on with the rest of her application in much the same vein, taking out her desperate sounding responses and replacing with Kaylie as femme-fatale; the kind of woman I'd pick if I was looking on a dating site.

Then I guffaw with laughter because I've never had the need to look on a dating site. I get so much pussy I'm surprised I've not been given charitable status as a pet rescue.

That does make me wonder who *does* look at

dating sites? I hope there is at least one normal bloke on there that can take my bestie out.

I realise that while I'm thinking of someone taking her on a date, I'm imagining the Kaylie I know, the frumpy one. But, if she were to make an effort...

A weird tight sensation occurs in my gut. Must be all the beer. I close down the laptop and I start thinking about curdled milk to take my mind off creamy tits. I wonder if hers actually look how they did in my dreams?

Oh God, what is happening to me?

I ROCK up to my sister's semi-detached house later that afternoon. The twins are five in December and are in their first year at school. She answers the door looking fraught and as I enter, I can hear the loud squeals and shouts of two small tearaways.

"Uncle Aiden is here." She yells, following with a whisper of, "*thank fuck.*" Two dark-haired, dark-eyed boys run through into the hall and throw themselves at me yelling my name.

I hold out my hands, each containing a Lego Duplo set.

"Go take these into the living room and I'll come help in a minute."

"We don't need help, Uncle Aiden. We're big boys." Thomas says, while Adam, who's a little quieter, nods his head vigorously.

"That's me told." I say to my sister as they run off.

"Come through to the kitchen and I'll make us both a hot drink."

"Coffee would be good. Extra spoonful in it please."

"Rough night?"

"Kay came over and we worked on her dating profile. I needed beer to survive."

Kay and my sister were friends—of course they'd also been in the same class—but they weren't close like we were. Steph had always been much more girly and very, very, bossy. So they were friends in that they'd chat like fishwives sometimes if Kay came to family events, but not enough that they met separately. She was *my* friend and Steph had always laughed about how protective I was over her.

"Kaylie got *you* to look at her dating profile? She must be desperate." She laughs as she pours water into two mugs.

"Well I am a hot-blooded male. I just told her she

needed to rid herself of the hobo look she had going on."

"And you're still *alive*?" Steph is wide-eyed.

"I gave her a lot of wine. Anyway, her profile is all updated now. I finished it this morning. Only I have to help her somehow. She was talking about sperm donation."

"She wants you to father her child? Oh my god, Aiden. How did you handle that? You know I always thought you two were a perfect match and just needed your heads banging together."

"STOP RIGHT THERE." I shout, shaking my head.

"No. She did not ask me to father her child. She just thought she might end up taking that route if things didn't work out in a natural way. That's why we decided to rework her dating application, so she can try to get a decent date. You know, Kay. She's not going to be happy with sperm donation. She wants all the hearts and flowers."

My sister's face dulls. "Yeah, well you don't always get that."

I walk over to her and hug her hard. "I know you don't. I know for you the journey was incredibly difficult; but Kay doesn't face difficulties in conceiving as far as we know. She just needs to put herself out there in the dating world more."

"Yeah, sorry."

"Don't be sorry. Look at what your journey brought you anyway. Worth every bit of the pain."

Steph beams. "They really were. Now, do you hear that?"

"Hear what?"

"Exactly. The sound of silence which no parent ever wants to hear because it means their kids are up to something."

We take our drinks into the living room to find they've unearthed Steph's Parlour Palm. It lays out of its pot across the carpet where the new Lego Duplo digger and farm set are making their home in it.

Steph turns to me sighing.

I shrug my shoulders.

"May as well let 'em carry on while we finish our drinks at least."

She nods. "Why not?"

My phone rings just as I'm about to take my seat. I switch my drink to my left hand and take it out from my pocket with my right.

Kaylie. I bet she's seen her profile and is calling to thank me.

I answer.

"Hey, Kay-bear."

"Do not 'hey Kay-bear' me. What the fuck have you done?" She screeches down the phone.

It's so loud even the boys hear it.

"That lady just said a really bad word." Adam looks disgusted and then he lifts the digger's scoop and blasts a load of soil onto the carpet.

Looking at my sister's face, I realise I'm in trouble with two women at the same time.

Well that's just fabulous.

"What's up?" I scratch at my chin wondering what I've done wrong.

"What's up?" she repeats. "I have seventeen responses already to my new profile."

"That's fantastic." I tell her but with how she says her next sentence in a slow drawn out, I-will-kill-you way, I guess I'm wrong.

"They all want to show me a good time. Every single application gives me either a description of their penis or asks me if I'm into some salubrious practices. I went to see what you'd done to my profile and there's no wonder. I sound like a hooker."

"I just made you..." I pause because I have to watch what I say in front of four-year-old ears. "More appealing?" I hedge.

"I'm currently sitting with my application trying to undo some of the damage. Seriously, Aiden. I thought you were supposed to be helping."

She ends the call.

I find my sister staring at me.

"What did you do now?"

"Can I borrow that?" I nod towards the digger. "Got myself in a bit of a hole, and not the ones I like." I wink.

5

KAYLIE

EVEN AS I'M staring at my new profile information that Aiden so helpfully edited for me, my notifications are blowing up.

I wonder how many more dick pics I can get in one day? I wonder. I've seen enough cocks today to last me a lifetime and I know for a fact that not one of them belongs to my future husband and father to my kids.

What the fuck was Aiden thinking making me sound like a desperate hooker who'd give it up for free?

I tap at my keys, although not hard enough to actually type anything, as I think.

Name: Kaylie Hale

Occupation: ~~Full time temptress.~~ Primary school teacher.

Age: ~~Old enough ;)~~ 29

Looking for: ~~Hot single man to treat me like a goddess.~~ A kind-hearted guy, who doesn't take life too seriously and is up for a little fun...

I PONDER the last one for the longest time. Does it still make me sound like a slut? Does Aiden have a point that I at least need to sound up for some fun myself to pull a decent guy? I almost delete it about a hundred times, but in the end, I decide to leave it for now and see what kind of response I get. I delete all the messages and notifications I received today because let's face it... they're all going to be dead ends.

Putting my phone on silent, I carry it through to the bathroom along with my large glass of wine for what I hope is going to be a very long and very relaxing bath.

It's Friday night. Any respectable twenty-nine-year-old should be out on the town enjoying themselves, but I just can't face it. Especially after the week I've had. My class had a head lice infestation. I lift my hand to scratch my head at the thought alone. It was also nativity planning week, letting the kids know what parts they'll be playing. I'm already looking forward to the unhappy parents' phone calls about how their little angel is wasted as a sheep or a donkey.

I shake my head in an attempt to remove the thoughts. School is done for the week, now it's time to relax.

I light a couple of my favourite candles and pour way too much bubble bath into the tub. The room fills with the scent of vanilla and cherry blossom. I feel my tense muscles start to relax from that alone.

Rushing back to my bedroom, I strip down to nothing and run back through the flat hoping that Cheryl and her boyfriend don't choose this exact moment to walk through the front door.

Thankfully, I make it without flashing anyone. Shutting and locking the door behind me, I reach for my phone and pull up my favourite playlist.

The water is a little too hot and it stings as I sink down into it, but I welcome it knowing it's to relax me and my body will acclimatise in a moment.

Resting back, I close my eyes and let my day

wash away. Vivid descriptions of men's cocks, actual photographs of men's cocks, and an array of propositions, some of which I had no clue what they were asking for, magically disappear.

I must fall asleep at some point because the next thing I know, I duck down a little and the water's cold.

"Fuck."

Sitting up, I make quick work of washing my hair and body. Pulling the plug, I climb out and reach for the towels.

"Bollocks." I fucking knew I'd forget that I put them in the wash before work this morning. Fuck, fuck, fuck.

I take my make-up off in the hope that by hopping from side to side to keep warm, I'll have drip-dried enough to run back to my bedroom by the time I've finished.

I'm fresh faced, slightly buzzed from my wine and dry enough not to leave soggy footprints through the house when I turn and flick the lock.

I listen for a few seconds to make sure no one's in the hallway before pushing the handle down and preparing for the quick sprint. Only when I pull the door, nothing happens.

What?

Assuming I did something wrong, although I'm not sure how I could open a door wrong, I try again.

Nothing.

Grabbing it with both hands, I pull with everything I have; only my feet aren't as dry as I thought they were and they slip out from under me, leaving me in a heap on the tiled floor.

"Owww," I complain as pain shoots up my spine.

Sitting in my own puddle of bath water, I run through my options.

Call for help or climb out of the window of our second floor flat and find help.

So really there's only one option.

I carefully get to my feed, kill the music that still playing on my phone and find Cheryl's number.

It rings and rings and eventually just goes to voicemail.

"Where the fuck are you? I'm stuck in the fucking bathroom." My phone beeps and I pull it from my ear. "Shit." Hanging up quickly, I stare at the one percent battery and rush to find my next option.

"Hey, Kay-bear. You forgiven—"

"Shut up, I need your help."

"You need—"

"I said shut up. I need rescuing, I'm stuck in—"

Beep beep beep.

"Fuuuuuuck," I cry just about refraining from throwing the damn thing across the room.

I try turning it on again as if it has some kind of magic power, but all I get is the empty battery sign simply flashing back at me obnoxiously.

Now what the hell do I do? Sit here waiting in the hope my mostly absent roommate comes home tonight? It's pretty unlikely because her and Rick seem to spend every weekend together. When she does show her face here it's usually weeknights when he's got to be up early for work.

My back hits the wall and I slide down until my arse hits the cold tiles. A shiver runs up my spine but other than huddle next to the towel rail, or re-run the bath and get back in, I'm pretty fucked right now. I've even drunk all my wine. *Why didn't I bring in the bottle?* Like that's the most pressing issue at this time.

I've no clue how much time has passed but I'm cold, hungry, and tired. I was hoping to be in my pyjamas, tucked up in bed with a soppy romance film on the TV and a tub of ice cream in my hands, yet here I am. Although, on the plus side, I now know that this bathroom has twelve floor tiles, of which only six are full tiles, and eighty-four wall tiles. And, I fucking hate them. Why anyone would choose this cream and burgundy floral design, fuck only knows.

When the cold gets too much, I climb from the floor and run the bath once again, hoping that it's been long enough for the hot water to refill. While I wait, I glance around the room for something else to do to pass the time.

I find one of Cheryl's facepacks that I always take the piss out of her for and rip the top open. If I'm going to die a slow and painful death, I might as well go out with clear pores.

My skin is pruned to within an inch of its life and the facepack has dried like fucking cement when I hear a noise like the front door opening.

"Hello," I scream, jumping up so fast that the bath water sloshes everywhere. "I'm in the bathroom. Help."

I don't hear anything else and I wonder if I'm starting to hallucinate but it's only a few more seconds before I hear the most blissful sound.

"Kaylie?"

"Aiden. Oh my god, you came."

"Yeah, well, when I came up empty in your usual restaurants of choice for disastrous dates I wasn't sure what else to do, so I figured you might have come home. My next option was the hospital in case tonight's date was a serial killer. I don't think you've met one of those yet." His chuckle bounces off the tiles around me and ignites an anger I'm unable to contain in my belly.

"Not the fucking time for jokes, Aid. I'm fucking stuck in here."

"You're stuck?"

"Yes. I need rescuing from my fucking bathroom, you moron."

"All right, enough of the abuse. Do you want help or not?"

"Yes, yes, I'm sorry. I really need your help. I'm stuck, with no towels, freezing my tits off."

"Really?" He sounds way too excited about this.

"Aiden. Focus. Get me out of here."

"Okay, stand back. I'll kick it down."

"What? No! You can't do that," I shout in panic.

"Why? You want to get out, don't you?"

"Yes, but I'd rather not be kicked out by my landlord for breaking down his door."

"You're stuck. What do you think he'd prefer? A dead body in the bathroom?"

"No, probably not," I mutter. "Can you get a screwdriver and let me out or something?"

"Do you have a screwdriver?"

"No."

"Fantastic. Any more shitty suggestions, or shall we just do what I said to begin with?"

I'm now shivering. "D- do you have to be enjoying this quite so much?"

"Yeah, I really do. Are you out of the way?"

"I'm standing in the bath. It's about as far away as I can get from a room that's barely six foot square."

"Okay, brace yourself."

I crouch down behind the shower curtain like it's going to protect me and wait for impact.

The first bang does nothing. The door is still in place and when Aiden pushes the handle it doesn't open.

"Stubborn little fucker," Aiden grunts before he must run at it full force. The sound of splintering wood fills the air before both him and the door come flying into the room. The door hits the sink, sending it crashing down to the floor, resulting in water spraying up into the room like a fancy fucking water feature while Aiden groans.

"Fuck, are you okay?"

Jumping up, I climb from the bath, but I don't get

any further because his eyes land on my body and I'm reminded that I'm stark bollock naked.

I wrap one arm around my boobs and drop the other to my crotch but it's too late. The heat in his eyes and the smirk playing on his lips tells me that he's already seen everything.

6

AIDEN

ANOTHER NIGHT. Another phone call from Kaylie. She's becoming as regular as my alarm clock.

"Hey, Kay-bear. You forgiven—"

"Shut up, I need your help."

"You need—"

"I said shut up. I need rescuing, I'm stuck in—"

There are a series of beeps and her phone goes dead. I wait for her to call me back with a location but there's nothing. Sighing, I scrub a hand through my hair and realise that I'm not lazing around on the sofa this Friday evening; instead, I'm out looking for Kay. Jeez, I meet her so often in restaurants we're practically dating ourselves.

But I don't find her in her usual haunts and there are only two restaurants she meets dates at: one main one, and a back-up if her original choice is fully booked. There's no sign of her and I start to worry that the call ended because the serial killer she was out with removed her phone. My heart starts to beat thick and fast. Fuck, has my messing with her dating account caused some random crazy dude to target her? What if she's missing? What if I never see her again?

Thank fuck for my regular gym attendance and training sessions because I run to her flat and use my keys to get in to find...

A body all right.

But not a dead one.

As I stand in front of her now, having kicked the door down, I'm looking at one very hot, very naked, body.

I can't help the smirk that catches my lips.

"Get me a towel or my robe, you fucking pervert," she screams at me. Her banshee tone is at a level of decibels that is going to threaten the glass in the bathroom window at any second.

"Personally, I'd have wrapped myself in the shower curtain." I nod at the black shower curtain hung in front of her and watch her eyes widen as she realises she could have been covered up if her brain hadn't failed her in her panic. She reaches out to grab

57

the bottom of the curtain to pull it all around her but shows me a breast while she does so.

It's not like the ones she had in my dreams. It's even better. She has just the perfect sized breasts I reckon, to cup in my hands, and I hadn't realised how much amazing junk she has in the trunk until the shower curtain clings to her rear.

"You do realise the shower curtain is attached right, so you're now stuck standing in the bath."

The withering look I get snaps me from my perving. "Well if you could quit checking me out and go get the towel or robe I asked you for five minutes ago, maybe I could get out of here. And go turn the stopcock off before the bathroom floods."

"With that black face mask on your face and wrapped in a black shower curtain I'm feeling all kinds of Catwoman vibes."

"You will if you don't GO GET ME A ROBE, because I'm going to scratch your fucking pervert eyes out in a minute."

"Jesus." I roll my eyes. "I'll go get you a robe AND sort the stopcock. Think you'd be more thankful for me coming to rescue you yet again. Can you imagine if you'd had to be rescued by the fire brigade? All your booty on show for the watch."

I get another withering stare and so leave the

bathroom.

After turning off the stopcock under the kitchen sink, I walk into Kaylie's bedroom realising I've not been in here before. It's decorated in a pale grey with grey everything apart from a couple of pink cushions. There's a sad looking single bed in her room and books everywhere. She always was a bookworm. I find a tatty burgundy-coloured towelling robe on the back of her door and walk back to the bathroom handing it to her.

"Thanks. Now go and put the kettle on and make me a nice cuppa so I can recover from this ordeal."

"Yes, Miss." I salute and with a last wistful look at the shower curtain clinging to her curves, I make my way back towards the kitchen. Luckily the kettle is still full of water from an earlier brew.

Right now, I want to be a shower curtain. My mind is full of naked Kaylie and my thoughts are not pure regarding my best friend. I don't know what to do about them, but right now they're forgiven as we have just seen her naked. I'm a hot-blooded male after all. My mind just needs to process the naked, and then I'm sure after I've spent time with my bestie all will return to normal.

She walks into the kitchen and flopping onto a

chair at the kitchen table, she sits with her head in her hands.

"I don't know what I've done to deserve all this shit," she whines.

I place her tea in front of her. "Kay-bear, there's no harm done. You got stuck in the bathroom and I rescued you. My payment was a look at that mighty fine body you've been hiding away all these years. Let me tell you, next time you go on a date you are dressing to accentuate that. It's time to stop wearing baggy oversized shit that does nothing for you and to show off the goods that God provided."

"I can't get the face pack off." She sighs heavily. "It's one of those I've laughed at on the internet. I thought the people on there had just made it up to get views." She pulls at the edge of the black mask and winces. "Nope, can't even lift the slightest bit of it. This is my new look for life."

"Don't be daft. They just wash off, don't they?"

"Aiden, have you not seen the video clips of these on the internet?"

I shake my head while on my phone I'm already typing in face mask removal on YouTube. A minute later I'm laughing. "Oh fuck. There's nothing you can do, Kaylie, but lift slowly and endure the pain by the looks of it."

"I'm well aware of the pain I'm going to have to go through." She stands up and goes into the pantry bringing out a bottle of vodka. "I'm not doing this sober," she says and begins pouring a large measure into a glass which she necks.

I can't blame the girl. My eyes are watering just from watching the clips on the internet. "I don't want to drink alone, Aid. Get drunk with me, will you? And I might cry if it's really painful. I don't have a high pain threshold at all."

Given she once stubbed her toe and fainted I already know this. She definitely needs booze to survive.

"Pass me the bottle."

An hour later, Kaylie's face mask is still on and we're both rat-arsed. So drunk that somehow I thought it was a good idea to put the face mask on myself because I'd decided it 'couldn't be as bad as she was making out' and I'd show her how a man handled it.

I was trying to ease the edge of the mask off now and my eyes were stinging with tears, big proper fat tears.

"I think I'm going to have to live like this, Kay-bear. But it's okay, cos if you keep yours on forever too then we won't look so odd. There's probably a whole heap of people who can't remove them. We can set up a support network."

"I'm tired and I want to go to bed so I'm doing it. I'm taking the motherfucker off." Kay slurs and she starts edging it off her face. For the next five minutes I have never heard language like it from my best friend, not even when I puked down her best dress at her sweet sixteenth. But off it is. I watch as she swigs another ton of vodka and applies aloe vera gel to her face. Her very pink face.

"Come on, your turn. Then we need to go to sleep and block out the pain." Kaylie moves her chair closer to mine and starts moving her hand near my face. I catch it in mine.

"Keep your hands to yourself," I snigger. "I'm always having to say that to women."

Kaylie sniggers back. "Don't think you'd be getting the same reaction from your fan club right now."

"I bet I still look hot."

"Yeah, a hot mess. Now come on, I want to go to bed. You can stay on the sofa."

"Oh no. I'm not staying on that disgusting thing that your flatmate's shagged on. I'll take this off if I can share your bed."

"I only have a single!"

"Oh yeah. Well, I don't care. I'll need you to hold me, Kay-bear, cos I'm going to be in a whole lot of pain. It's all right for you, women endure childbirth, you'll have a higher pain threshold. I only have to be nudged in a testicle and I think I might die."

"Fuck's sake. Fine." She pours me another vodka and puts it in front of me. "That's for after." Before I can think she's yanked the mask from my chin exposing half of my cheek.

"Holy fucking mother of cunting God." I leap up from the chair wafting air at my burning cheek.

Fuck.

Shit.

Fuck.

Bastard.

"Holy Christ, I think I'm gonna faint, Kay."

"We need to carry on, Aid. It's the only way."

I'm full on trembling as I sit back down on the chair. "As fast as you can and I apologise in advance for all my language and if I accidentally punch you to get you to stop."

And then the most painful minutes of my life occur, and I've run a marathon at that.

I'm full on crying. The vodka has done seemingly nothing to dull the pain. "Who made this stuff?" I appeal to my friend.

"I don't know, but I think we should put it in the bin."

"It needs to be given to MI5 for when they're interviewing terrorists. They'd get every secret ever in just a twitch of the mask."

We make our way to bed and I fall onto Kaylie's single and then I don't remember anymore.

Except I wake the next morning, my skin still sensitive and a little sore, and my head a lot sorer. Thank goodness I'm not back at work until tomorrow. I wonder where Kaylie is. Maybe fixing our breakfast? It's a shame I don't remember us sharing the bed. I wonder if we spooned?

I hear the weirdest noise and I realise it's the sound of heavy snoring. I get out of bed noticing I'm still fully clothed and follow the noise. Her flatmate's room is ajar and I find Kaylie in her robe laid diagonal across the double bed. Her robe has come undone and she's exposing her boobs and bush to the world. I have a decent look for a minute or two. I'm male, how many more times? Then I walk over and pull her robe across her covering her modesty. She groans but doesn't wake.

Then I go and make myself a shit ton of coffee.

7

KAYLIE

BY THE TIME I finish in the bathroom, Aiden is flat out on his back, snoring and taking up almost every inch of my pathetic single bed. Because if my life as a spinster isn't constantly on my mind, I always have my bed for one to remind me that I have no one to cuddle me at night. I have two options, the sofa, which Aiden already helpfully reminded me I'd caught Cheryl at it on more than once, with not just her current boyfriend; or her bed. It smells like the sheets have been washed since she last slept here, another reason why I think she's secretly moved out.

I fall on her bed, avoiding getting between the sheets just in case I'm wrong about them being clean.

The image of Aiden staring at my naked body

runs through my mind before I fall asleep. I can't help wondering what he really thought. If he was just saying what he thought I'd want to hear, or if he actually meant what he said.

The next morning, I wake to the smell of coffee flowing through the flat. My eyes flutter open and I wince at the amount of light shining through the open curtains.

Shoving my face into the pillow, my head pounds from the amount of vodka we consumed and I wince in pain and sit up.

"What the—" I gingerly touch my fingertips to my cheeks as the memory of the fucking face mask disaster hits me. Did anything go right last night?

"Morning," I say, hesitantly walking into my own kitchen. Heat floods my face, not that I'm sure he'd notice seeing as it's still glowing and missing a layer of skin. I've no idea if things will be awkward between us after last night. We definitely ventured into territory our friendship hasn't been exposed to before.

"Morning, Kay-bear. How are you feeling?"

"Give me coffee. Strong, please."

"That good?" he chuckles.

"I've no idea if I said it last night but thank you for rescuing me... again."

"Trust me, the pleasure was all mine."

"If we could please never mention it ever again that would be awesome."

He makes a show of zipping his lips shut and throwing away the key like we used to do when we told each other secrets as kids, but the amusement still shining in his eyes makes me question if he's telling the truth or not.

Aiden stays long enough for me to cook him bacon butties and then he heads off home before spending the rest of the morning sweating at the gym while I sit about and wait for an emergency plumber to fix the smashed sink and pipes in the bathroom. I phoned my landlord first thing, apologised profusely, and explained that I'd get it fixed ASAP. I know it's not really my fault that the door got stuck but he's already threatened to kick us out once before. I don't want to give him a legit reason to do it again.

Once he's finished and I have a working bathroom once again, minus a door for now, I take my sore and glowing face into town to make a start on my Christmas shopping.

I have a list but my biggest frustration every year is my brother. He has everything he could possibly need and enough money in case he remembers something he forgot to buy. Now he's got a wife and a baby on the way. The lucky fucker really does have everything. Jealousy licks at my insides but I refuse to let it fester. Jenson's had a tough few years what with his bitch of an ex-wife, and I can't deny that he hasn't worked his arse off to get his restaurant to where it is now.

I just sit down for lunch with a giant cappuccino and a panini when my phone vibrates in my pocket.

Swiping at the notification from the dating app, up pops a photo of a really good-looking guy.

"Now that's more like it," I mutter to myself, much to the amusement of the table next to me. *I bet he doesn't smell like rotten cabbage.*

Name: Brett Mathews

Occupation: Paediatric nurse

Age: 32

Looking for: Something meaningful with a hint of fun

Not wanting him to find someone else in the seconds since he showed an interest in me, I give him a like and place my phone on the table in front of me, trying to not stare at it while hoping I might get a message.

I'm halfway through my panini when it lights up.

I scramble to grab it and end up flipping it up in

the air in my haste. Thankfully, I catch it before it hits the floor.

Brett89: Hey, Beautiful. Would love to take you out for a bit of fun. Are you free tonight?

The fact he's mentioned 'fun' in his first message breaks one of my rules when it comes to meeting guys online, but after talking to Aiden about it all, I decide to throw caution to the wind and agree on an impromptu date tonight. I send him the address of my usual restaurant and agree to meet him at eight.

I forgo the rest of my shopping trip and head to a hairdressers instead, seeing as my roots are well overdue.

When I get home, I double lock the front door. If Cheryl comes home then she'll have to ring me to get in. I'm not showering without a bathroom door and giving anyone else a shot of my naked arse. It's bad enough that I could see something different in Aiden's eyes every time he looked at me after the traumatic ordeal that was last night's bath mishap.

Standing with a towel around my body and a

shower cap on my freshly coloured hair, I stare at the contents of my wardrobe.

Aiden's words about my shit, baggy clothes ring in my ears and I second guess my choice. Pulling the towel tighter around me, I walk into Cheryl's room and pull open her wardrobe. We're a similar build, and although Cheryl's boobs are quite obviously smaller than mine, I'm pretty sure her stuff will fit.

I push a few hangers along the rail until I come to a simple black wrap dress. It's understated, what I hope is sexy, and it doesn't look like it'll cling too bad.

After digging in the back of my underwear drawer, I find something that suits the dress and pull everything on.

I'm standing in front of my mirror trying to convince myself that the low V at my cleavage isn't too much when my phone pings.

Hotstuff: Photo of his still pink face. **How's the face?**

KaylieH: Currently being covered in make-up for a hot date.

Hotstuff: Pouting face. **Photo please.**

"Ugh pain in the arse."

Holding my phone at arms-length, I take what I hope is a flattering photo and send it over.

Hotstuff: Thumbs up photo. **Where do I need to rescue you from tonight?**

KaylieH: Middle finger photo. **I won't need it. Got a good feeling about this one. Check out the dress...**

I snap another picture of my outfit and send it over.

Hotstuff: Holy shit, Kay-bear. I think I just came in my pants.

Shaking my head at my idiot best friend, I throw my phone back on the bed and finish off my hair and make up before ordering an Uber to get me to my usual restaurant of choice.

BRETT IS WAITING for me with a single rose in his hand when I get there. My eyes almost pop out of my head as I take in his expensive looking slim grey trousers and perfectly pressed white shirt complete with a skinny tie. His hair is perfect; so perfect it makes me want to go to the bathroom and smooth mine out. He's way too attractive to be spending the night with me.

"Wow, Kaylie. You're even more beautiful in real life."

He leans in to kiss my cheek and I have a cheeky sniff. I almost sing with delight when all I smell is the delicious scent of freshly washed man.

This night is really looking up.

We're directed to our table and when the waiter asks if we want wine, Brett double checks my preference before ordering a bottle of my favourite French white.

"Good choice. I went to Chardonnay a few years ago. If you ever get the chance you must go wine tasting there. It was incredible... well, what I remember of it."

"You're not meant to actually swallow it are you?"

"I'm not a fan of spitting. You?"

Redness stains my cheeks but unlike almost

every other guy I've dated, the way Brett just said that wasn't sleazy in any way. It was just cheeky, and I can't deny it's kickstarted tingles low down in my belly that I haven't felt in a very, very long time.

"Wine? Never. Such a waste."

"My point exactly."

The waiter returns and pours us both a glass before Brett lifts his and makes a toast.

"To our first date. Hopefully the first of many."

I'm getting such good feelings about this guy, but a huge part of me is waiting for the ball to drop and for him to reveal a really ugly secret that's going to turn me right off.

But that never happens. We talk about our lives, our jobs, our hobbies, and our mutual hope of moving out of the city one day to live in the country.

It's hands down the best date I've ever had. So obviously something has to go wrong.

We're on dessert, which I'm secretly hoping is a prelude to another kind of dessert that we might partake in back at my flat when a shadow falls over our table.

"Kaylie, what the hell are you doing? I didn't believe it when Jenson said you were out on a date. How could you? We only agreed on having a break this morning yet you're already here getting your claws into another guy. And to think... we were meant to be getting married. Thank God there's still time to get my deposit back on the venue."

The sound of Brett's chair scraping against the wooden floor eventually stops Aiden's bullshit long enough for me to get a word in.

"Brett, he's joking. He's not—"

"I thought maybe you were different from all the other slags on that site. Guess I was wrong." And with that, Brett's gone, along with any hopes of me getting any action tonight.

"You fucking idiot. What the hell did you do that for? I was having a great time. He was actually someone I wanted to spend some time with."

Guilt twists Aiden's face but it's not as genuine as he wants me to believe.

"You're paying the fucking bill, dickhead."

I push my chair out behind me and storm towards the toilets. I take about six steps before I realise there's still a forkful of chocolate torte on my plate. Fuck that, it's bad enough my dates gone awry, I'm not missing out on chocolate. I rush back and fork it into my mouth, refusing to meet Aiden's eyes, and then I stomp off again. It's that or stab Aiden in the eye with my previously mentioned dessert fork.

I forego the cubicles as I don't actually need to

use the facilities, in favour of leaning my palms on the marble counter and staring at myself in the mirror.

"Did you really think you'd have a successful date for once?"

My nails try digging into the stone as anger radiates through my veins. How dare Aiden show up unannounced and ruin everything. I gave him no sign that my date was going south. Is he just so used to coming to my rescue that he couldn't leave me be?

Telling myself that I need to stop leaning on my best friend so much to get myself out of bad situations, I leave the toilets, ready to head home alone once again.

Aiden's sitting in Brett's seat when I walk back out into the restaurant but with fire burning in my belly, I turn towards the exit to escape.

8

AIDEN

THERE HASN'T BEEN a call to come to her rescue.

I'm sitting on the sofa, my feet tapping. I don't know how many times I've checked my phone.

I've turned into a needy girl.

Maybe I'm having some kind of a mental breakdown? I mean, I keep thinking of my best friend not like a best friend. I can't get her body out of my mind. The body she's taken on a date tonight and...

THERE'S BEEN NO CALL.

I know something is desperately wrong with my psyche when I decide that her being held hostage by some strange serial killer sits better in my mind than her actually being on a successful date.

Without giving things any further thought, I jump up, grab my car keys and head straight for the restaurant she usually takes her dates to.

When I walk through the door, nodding to the staff who by now have worked out that I'm either Kaylie's wingman or we have some strange sex game going on, I stop in my tracks as I see her eating dessert and some dude talking to her, all charm and just. Fucking. NO.

I know what dessert leads to. I need to stop this. She needs time to think about this. She's not putting out on a first date. He is not getting his smooth lecherous hands on my girl.

My girl?

Obviously I mean that in terms of her being my best friend forever, right?

I'm looking out for my best friend. That. Is. All.

I stomp over to their table. A look of horror hits Kaylie's face and she's shaking her head in a 'no, I don't need this' way but I'm here now and this is happening. I'm like a runaway train about to crash through an unknown new destination.

"Kaylie, what the hell are you doing? I didn't believe it when Jenson said you were out on a date. How could you? We only agreed on having a break this morning yet you're already here getting your claws into another guy. And to think... we were meant to be getting married. Thank God there's still time to get my deposit back on the venue."

Her date's face turns into a sneer as he pushes back his chair.

"Brett, he's joking. He's not—"

Brett? What kind of fucking name is that? Sounds as oily as he is. Kaylie is not ending up with a Brett. Their couple name would be BreKay which sounds like our shortened form of breakfast, brekkie. It's lame and she's having no part in any 'breakfast' situations with Brett the dickhead.

"I thought maybe you were different from all the other slags on that site. Guess I was wrong." Brett fucks off. Result. I'm happier than when I finished that marathon that time. I could punch the air right now. But Kaylie's expression means I tone it down.

"You fucking idiot. What the hell did you do that for? I was having a really good time. He was actually someone I wanted to spend some time with."

A little bit of guilt hits my face because after a series of shit dates my bestie was actually having a good time, but I can't help it, a smirk twitches at my lips. I have no poker face, never have, and my best friend knows every expression I have in my repertoire anyway.

"You're paying the fucking bill, dickhead."

She storms towards the women's bathroom, although it makes me laugh because she comes back to shovel in her last morsel of chocolate torte first, the chocoholic. I'm standing there wondering what to do when a waitress comes over. I can tell from her face that although she's pretending to enquire if I want to order anything, she's actually here representing all the restaurant staff who are dying to know what's happening.

"Can I have a beer? Also, I'd better pay the bill, because I might have to leave at super quick notice."

"I know this isn't very professional of me," the waitress says. "But for what it's worth, I think she's a fool not to realise that you are perfect for her."

"Oh, er, no, she's just my best friend. I'm her wingman."

The waitress flushes. "Oh, I'm sorry. It's just we've all seen how you look so perfect together. We thought maybe you were like her knight in shining armour. I'll shut up now, because I'm embarrassing myself. It's just... no, shut up, Lisa."

"No, carry on. What were you going to say?"

"Well, you always look so happy when you leave with her. We've been rooting for you to get the girl and every time she comes in with someone else, we think oh she's still not seen what's right in front of her."

I nod. "Okay. Seriously, thanks for your honesty, it's appreciated."

She nods. "I'll get you that bill and your beer."

I pay my bill and I drink my beer wondering if Kaylie has gone through a window and home. The restaurant staff think I'm some guy with a crush. I look happy every time her dates go wrong. What the fuck is wrong with me?

I think my brain is going to admit something to me that I'm not prepared to hear.

You've been happy that Kaylie's dates have all gone to shit.

You were happy when her long-term relationship with Phillip went to shit.

You are a shit.

And you're in love with your best friend.

I sink the whole lot of my beer down.

Why the fuck can you not take out your brain and leave it in a cloakroom when it's doing your head in?

Face facts. Face facts. Face facts.

You love Kaylie Hale.

But it doesn't matter. It doesn't matter that I have feelings for this woman. If I tried to pursue things...

If it got fucked up... Then I wouldn't have my best friend anymore. The best friend I've had since I was six years old. So unrequited love here I come, because this can never happen.

I'm fucked.

And in a completely unsatisfying way.

The restaurant staff know it.

Has anyone else noticed? Oh God, does my sister suspect? We're so close, we know everything about each other's feelings, usually without even having to ask.

I have no time to think about things any further because Kaylie comes out of the toilets and rushes straight for the exit. Good job I paid the bill.

"Kaylie, wait up."

She rounds on me and in front of all the staff she tells me to go fuck myself. I shrug my shoulders at Lisa as I leave. I bet we're more entertaining than EastEnders. Kaylie is off out of the door and stomping down the street. It's okay, she's heading in the right direction for the car park. I just need to get her to stop by the end of the street.

"Kaylie. I'm sorry. I thought you needed rescuing like usual. That guy looked shady."

She stops and swings back around to me and she swings her bag at me. Full on swings that small handbag that weighs a fucking ton and it hits me right in the eye.

"Fuuuccccckk."

"Oh my god. Sorry. I meant to aim for your chest."

I'm clutching my eye in severe pain. "What have you got in there?"

"My usual date stuff. Purse, mobile, keys, rape alarm, hammer."

"You have a *hammer* in there?"

"Yeah, I date strangers. I need to be able to protect myself."

"Well, we know you'll be fine because you've probably blinded me." I'm still clutching at my face and I feel a bit faint, so I sit on the floor with my back against the wall of the phone shop a few doors down from the restaurant.

People walk past us and I hear complaints about 'people who can't handle their beer'. They don't realise I've been attacked by the hottie kneeling down next to me. Even with one eye I can see her amazing rack in that wrap dress.

She takes hold of my hand. "Take your hand away and let's look at the damage." Slowly, we peel my hand away from my eye. It's all a bit blurred from where my hand was pressing, but slowly my perfect eyesight is revealed. Thank God. However, feeling around just above my eye socket it's swollen and hurts like a sharp kick to the bollocks.

"Oh shit, it's bruising. I'm so sorry, Aiden. However, I can't help but think it's karma for fucking up my date."

"He looked shady."

"He was lovely and I hadn't phoned for you to rescue me."

"I thought either you'd been kidnapped or that your phone had run out of juice. You never have a successful date; it's not my fault I panicked."

"Get up, you complete moron." Kaylie says, holding out a hand, which makes me smile because there's no way she'd be able to pull me to my feet.

"Thanks, but I can get up. Would you mind just moving away slightly so that swinging handbag can't fuck up my other eye?"

"Ooops."

"My car's in the usual spot. Let me drive you home and I'll apologise all the way back." I tell her, though I know my whole conversation will be me lying because I'm so fucking happy I fucked it all up.

"Aiden…"

"Yup."

"Why are you smiling like a lunatic? You've

upset me, ruined my date, and have a black eye. Did I also hit your head?"

"I'm just so happy you're still talking to me," I lie.

"Always, even if you're a complete fucktard, you're my bestie." She shoves me in the arm as we walk.

Her bestie.

Her best friend.

If I cry now can I blame my eye?

"I really am so sorry," I lie on the journey back to hers.

She sighs. "It's okay. He was a bit slimy to tell you the truth."

Ha!

"But it did give me hope because I enjoyed the date that there is someone out there for me, so it wasn't all bad. Plus, I got as far as dessert and that chocolate torte was fucking-A."

We pull up outside her place and the lights are on.

"Oh God, looks like the lovebirds are home."

"You can come stop at mine if you like?" I offer, feeling hope that I can spend more time with her.

"No, it's okay. I need to catch Cheryl in the morning and ask her what's going on and if she's planning on moving out because that obviously has implications for me."

"Sure, okay."

I'm bitterly disappointed. I cannot lie.

She gets out of the car. "Speak tomorrow?"

"Yeah, I'm working, but we'll catch up at some point. Night, Kaylie."

"Can you believe it's my thirtieth birthday next Saturday? Jesus, Aiden, where has all the time gone? Good job we didn't make one of those 'if we're not married by thirty' deals or you'd be shitting a brick right now, Mr Manwhore."

Now my stomach is in my shoes. Is this what she sees when she looks at me? And why am I wishing we'd made one of those pacts. Goddamn it younger me, you fucked up big time there. Fuckhead.

"How's the eye?" She adds.

"It'll be a lot better the sooner I get some ice on it, so I'd better head off. Night, Kay-bear."

"Night, Aiden."

I DON'T THINK things can possibly get any worse until I receive a text when I'm home from work Monday night.

Kay-bear: You are never going to guess who started work at my school today.

Aiden: One of your disastrous dates?

Kay-bear: Close. Phillip. He's back in town and has taken a temporary post in the hope it leads to something permanent. He's asked me for a coffee after work as he wants to clear the air given we've got to work together.

I throw the phone down on the bed as if it's a hairy assed spider and I'm an arachnophobe.

Her ex. The person she thought was her happy ever after has come back.

Fuck. My. Life.

9

KAYLIE

I WANTED to hold a grudge and be mad at Aiden for ruining my one and only decent date on Saturday night but in reality, I couldn't.

Almost every date up until this weekend I've leant on him to rescue me when things have gone wrong. I guess I can't really blame him for expecting this date to go south as well. It would have just been nice of him to test the water before he came barrelling in with his dramatics.

It's weird to hear someone else moving around in the flat when I close the door behind me. I walk the short distance to Cheryl's room to find pretty much what I was expecting. Her packing her remaining stuff.

"Shit, Kay. You scared me. I wasn't expecting you home yet."

"So what, you were going to pack up and leave and not tell me?" Irritation floods me that after all the years we've been roommates she'd even consider doing something so shitty.

"What? No. Of course I was going to tell you." She rolls her eyes at me like I'm being overly dramatic but I find it hard to agree with her.

"So you're finally leaving then? What about the rent and giving notice?"

"I'm paid up until the end of next month so that should give you plenty of time to find a replacement."

I fume. I don't want to have to find another roommate; it was hard enough finding Cheryl. I should be the one organising to find a new place to live. I should be the one moving on with a boyfriend. But here I am, almost thirty and totally alone.

"Right, well... that's great. Thanks for the warning." Turning, I storm towards my room.

"I'm sorry, Kaylie." Sounds out behind me but I don't stop. I'm already over tonight.

I spend almost all of Sunday working before I sit with my laptop to see if I could possibly afford a decent place by myself or if I'm going to be forced to attempt to find a normal roommate. Truthfully, I'm not overly confident about my ability to do so seeing as I can barely find a decent human to have a meal with let alone live with.

I'm desperate to phone Aiden to find out what he thinks I should do, but knowing he's at work and that I need to stop relying on him for every little thing that goes wrong in my life, I refrain from reaching out. I need to start acting my age and fix problems myself. All those intentions fly out the window the second I walk into the staff room the next morning because my need for my best friend's honesty is required more than ever.

EVERY MONDAY MORNING is staff briefing before we settle into a week full of classes, snotty noses, and tantrums.

I'm sitting in my usual spot with my head in my diary looking at the week ahead when someone falls down onto the chair beside me. I usually don't take that much notice, preferring to live inside my own little bubble, but there's something so familiar about the scent that fills my nose, I'm forced to drag my head up and look.

When I do my eyes almost pop out of my head.

"Hello, Kaykay. How are you?"

My chin drops as I run my eyes over every inch of my ex's face. It's been what... five... no six years since he decided one day that the settled life of a long-term relationship wasn't for him and that he wanted to sow his wild oats.

"What the hell are you doing here?"

"It's nice to see you too."

I haven't laid eyes on Phillip since the day he walked out of the flat we shared, and to be honest, I kind of expected it to stay that way for the rest of my life. I'd have been more than happy with that too. Jesus, I thought the man staring at me now with a couple of lines around his eyes and a slightly receding hairline was it for me. I truly believed that we were meant to be and at almost twenty-four I was waiting for the engagement ring I'd been dreaming of coming at any moment. He knew my goals. I wanted to be married and have at least one baby by the time I was thirty. He always said he agreed, but then suddenly he claimed to want the total opposite and was gone faster than I could blink, leaving me in a flat I couldn't afford. The similarity to my current situation isn't lost on me. I guess I should just be glad that my heart isn't involved this time around. Phillip's disappearing act was what led me to find Cheryl in the first place, so I guess it's ironic that the day after she walks out of my life, he walks back in.

"I'd love to say the same, Phillip, but I'm not really feeling all that great about it."

His shock is evident on his face. He knew me as a meek and mild little mouse. He used to tell me to jump and I'd immediately ask how high. Aiden had been telling me throughout the relationship that I was losing myself, but it wasn't until Phillip left that I was able to acknowledge just how much he'd been controlling me. Even to this day I would argue that it was unintentional on his part but sitting here right now and looking him in the eye once again, I'm not so sure.

"Good morning, happy campers," our headteacher sings, officially starting our new week.

While I keep my eyes on him and attempt to focus on what he has to tell me, Phillip keeps his eyes on me. They burn into the side of my head. My nails dig into the cushioning under my arse in an attempt to keep myself in my seat. All I want to do is run. Run and hide in my classroom until I'm able to lock myself in my flat and try to figure out how the fuck I'm meant to look him in the face without wanting to pull my hammer out of my bag. After Saturday night, I already know it's pretty efficient.

Guilt washes through me as I think about the black eye selfie I woke up to this morning. I never meant to cause Aiden any damage, I just wanted to express how pissed off I was.

"I'd like to welcome Phillip Harrington to the team. He's here as Laura's maternity cover for the next few months. I think he's going to be a great asset here so please make him welcome."

Irritation burns through me, my shoulders tense and my teeth grind. The second we're dismissed I'm out of there like someone lit a fire under my arse.

My morning continues as it started, some little darling has an accident, leaving a warm little puddle on the chair and the floor and while my PA is out dealing with him, another kid projectile vomits across the desk causing all hell to break loose.

The second the last little terror leaves for lunch, I drop my head to my desk. I need a do over on today. The last thing I need right that second is to hear his voice.

"How's your morning been, Kaykay?"

"Can you stop calling me that? I hated it back in the day and I still hate it now. And seeing as you asked, my morning's been shit, and to be honest, it isn't exactly looking up. What do you want?"

He looks a little wounded by my words and I just about manage to smile in delight.

"I wanted to come and apologise for how I treated you. I was out of order."

"You think?" I ask dryly.

"I just got scared. We were so young, Kayk—" He stops himself when my eyes narrow in frustration. "I just wasn't ready for all that. We'd been together since uni and I stupidly thought I was missing out being tied down already. I wanted to have the chance to experience what else was out there."

"And how was that for you?"

"Meh. I soon realised what I'd thrown away."

"Clearly you didn't miss it that much seeing as you just said you realised quite quickly yet you're standing here now, six years later, by total coincidence. If you're expecting me to give you another chance then you're really going to have to try better than that."

"So are you single? I noticed you're not wearing a ring." Hope shines in his eyes, making me wonder for the first time if we were just too young back then and things could be good between us once again. But would I want that?

"Yes, I'm single," I say through gritted teeth.

"Let me take you out for coffee after work. I want to show you that I'm not the man you remember. I've grown up since our time together."

"So have I, Phillip."

"I can see that. Say yes?"

Blowing out a breath, I figure that agreeing might get him out of my classroom faster so I can eat and hide for a few minutes before the kids reappear.

"Fine. There's a coffee shop around the corner. I'll meet you out the front after school."

A giant smile lights up his face and my stomach drops. Did I just give him the wrong idea?

Thankfully the afternoon involves no bodily fluids and before I know it the bell rings signalling the end of the first day of the week. With only a few weeks to go before Christmas, the kids are starting to get a little hyper with the approaching Santa visit. The next few weeks are going to be exhausting, even more so if I have to spend that time trying to avoid my ex.

As promised, he's waiting patiently for me out the front when I eventually arrive. I must admit, I was dragging my heels a little to get out here in the hope he might get fed up, but it looks like I'm not going to be that lucky.

"Hey," I say walking up behind him. "I'm ready for the caffeine fix."

"Me too. I forgot how hard the first day at a new school is."

I mumble my agreement, but in reality this has been my one and only school. "Did you know I still worked here?"

"I... um..."

"Did you come here for me, Phillip?"

"That's one of the reasons. That and my parents aren't getting any younger. Figured it was time to come home."

I don't really know how I feel about this sudden reappearance and interest after six years of radio silence. I can't help but think there's more to it. He can't have suddenly woken up one morning and decided he missed me so much that he had to get a job at my school. Probably wants to marry me so I'll look after his parents for him. Oh God. I bet I'm right!

Once we get to the front of the queue, he takes it upon himself to order what he remembers as my usual and it pisses me off that he'd just assume.

"I can order for myself, you know?"

"Oh yeah. Sorry. Force of habit."

"After six years?"

This is what I need. The reminder of why he wasn't actually that good for me.

We find ourselves a table and silence falls around us. An uncomfortableness that hasn't been present during our other interactions today is suffocating.

"So how have you been? What have you been up to?"

The thought of explaining everything I've done over the past six years doesn't sound very inviting so I cut it right down.

"Oh, not a lot. Working mainly, spending time with Aiden and my family."

"Aiden's still about then, huh?" His lips purse as he says Aiden's name and it pisses me off.

"Yeah. Why'd you say it like that?"

"No reason."

I stare at his face, trying to see if old feelings for him still linger inside me. There might be a little something but I'm not really sure if it's feelings or just a little bit of nostalgia. I was angry for a long time after he left me, but at some point over the past few years, I realised he wasn't really worth it and moved on. If I cared, surely I'd still be angry, or feel something more than I do at least.

He insists on getting us a second drink seeing as our trip down memory lane has resulted in two empty cups and I excuse myself to visit the toilets. Pulling my phone from my bag, I consider an Aiden rescue but this is my mess that I need to get out of. Instead, I message him with an update on my day because he's really not going to believe this.

10

AIDEN

EVEN RESCUING a young cat from a tree in front of a women's football team doesn't cheer me up today. Even though it was so cold there were a lot of pebbled nipples. All I could think about was Kaylie and *him*.

Phillip the knobsack.

My time with my best friend had been severely limited when she'd dated him because he didn't like me. In fact, he didn't like anyone being around her who wasn't him. In hindsight he'd put my bestie in a gilded cage. He'd treated her fine. Just within his rules for life and boy did he have a lot. Thought he was someone special did Phillip.

And then after promising her the earth he just fucked off, saying he was too young. Left her with a broken heart and a flat she couldn't afford. He wanted me around then. All he had to say was 'go and see Aiden. He'll support you to get over me'.

Dipshit.

I keep picking my phone up when I get the chance but there are no more messages. It's six pm and I'm just about to walk in my front door. They're probably still out. Shall I text her?

No. Look what happened last time.

Back off.

I have to realise that my bestie is almost thirty years old. A grown woman who can make her own choices, whether they're good or ridiculous. I just have to trust she's not taken in by the BS that comes out of his mouth.

I walk into the house to find my roomie Brandon has all the downstairs curtains closed and is snoring on the sofa. The smell of morning breath and fusty body is all over the place.

I pick up a cushion and throw it at his head.

There's a groan and then he moves his head with a vacant 'where am I?' look on his face.

"Time'sit?" slips out of the side of his mouth.

"Time you slept in your actual bedroom, given that's what it's for, and maybe had a shower. You stink."

He sits up a bit and looks at me through sleepy eyes that keep closing. "What bit your arse?"

"I'm just fed up of you slobbing about, mate. What if I'd brought a girl back with me and we found you there?"

He shrugs his shoulders. "Just take them past me upstairs."

"God, you're such a lazy fucker. And it's almost ten past six."

Another groan. "I'm back at work in a couple of hours." He runs a hand through his shaggy, chin-length hair. "I need another job. I can't do this much longer. It's killing me."

"You say that on a daily basis but then when I hand you your laptop at the jobs page you say you can't be arsed, so suck it up, go get a shower and I'll order us some pizza on your credit card because I can see otherwise your turn on the food rota is not going to go well.

I watch as he rolls onto the floor and then stands up. It's like that evolution of man picture you see, though the actual human won't appear until after his shower.

An hour later we're back on the sofa that I've sprayed with my aftershave. All the windows have been opened and now the only odour is that of the gorgeous pizza we're tucking into.

Brandon's hair is now washed and combed back. He hasn't bothered shaving. But he pays his half of the rent on time and causes no trouble. I met Brandon in the gym a few years back, believe it or not. He managed to go for a whole week before giving up. During that week he'd spent more time chatting and putting me off my routine than working out, and mentioned he was looking to move out of his parents while asking to borrow my shower gel.

"So what's up with you? You've a face like a slapped arse."

I chuck my half-eaten pizza slice back in the box. I can't even eat right now. "It's Kaylie. Her ex has come back to town and she's gone for a coffee with him. He's a controlling arsehole. I want to storm the coffee shop and put my fist through his face."

"How'd you get the eye?"

"Now you notice my eye. Do you walk around in an actual coma?"

"Just didn't seem all that important. Figured it'd be the boyfriend of one of your women. Bound to happen at some point."

"Kaylie hit me. By accident."

"Fucking hell. You don't need to worry about her with this guy then if that's the punch she has on her."

"She hit me with a hammer."

Brandon's mouth drops open.

"It was in her handbag; it's a long story and right now we're focusing on the fact she's out with her dickhead ex."

"And you're jealous cos you want to bang her yourself."

"No."

"Yes."

"I do not want to bang Kaylie."

"Mate, it's about time we had this girly chat. You've had the horn for this girl as long as I can remember. You talk about her ALL THE TIME. You've stopped picking up women, because when you're not working you sit in at night waiting to go rescue her from her dates. You're totally pussy-whipped. It's time to admit the truth."

I take a deep breath.

"Okay. I only just noticed this week that she has a banging body and that well, I think I actually might love her."

Wide eyes and another repeat of the open mouth greets me.

"Excuse me?"

"I think I love her." I confess.

"I was expecting an 'I want to fuck her brains out'. Did the hammer hit you hard in the head or have I really just heard Mr Aiden Thomson declare himself in love?"

"Leave me alone."

"Unfortunately I have to because I've got to get ready for work, but fucking hell, mate. I am proper gobsmacked. You need to do something then before she takes that tool back and marries him."

"I know." I groan. "But she's my best friend. What if it goes wrong and I lose her?"

"You think if she marries someone else and has their babies you're not going to lose her anyway to a large extent? Can you manage an occasional quick phone call in between her chasing a toddler around the place? Can you imagine her pregnant with another man's child?"

He doesn't wait for an answer. He just clasps my shoulder on his way out, gives it a squeeze and leaves me to it.

It's nine pm when I get a text.

Kay-bear: You still at work? Banging a chick? You're very quiet today.

God, what do I put? I ponder for a moment.

Hot stuff: Been having pizza with Brandon. Just tired. Had to rescue a cat today. The tree was a big un.

Kay-bear: You complaining being around pussy? That's a new one.

Hot stuff: Maybe I've gone allergic...

Kay-bear: You okay?

Hot stuff: Yeah. Like I said... tired.

Kay-bear: I'll let you sleep.

Hot stuff: No, body tired, not brain tired. How'd coffee go?

Kay-bear: It was okay. It's like he doesn't realise any time has passed at all. Like he thinks he can pick up where we left off.

Hot stuff: Did you tell him to fuck off?

Kay-bear: No because I have to work with the guy for the next few months so I need to keep things civil. Also, what if there is still something there? I don't want to dismiss him after just a coffee. We were good once.

No you weren't. I think, but I type instead...

Hot stuff: So what's next?

Kay-bear: He asked me out to dinner, so I'm going to do that. Spend a bit more time with him, see how I feel. I don't think we have a future, but I need to gather more evidence. I know one thing though...

Hot stuff: What's that?

Kay-bear: All these dates and wasted time. That's what it all is. Wasted time. I wanted three kids, Aid. Three. I'm almost thirty. It's days away. If this is another

closed avenue then I'm doing the sperm donation. I wanted to conceive romantically by candlelight, but you know what, I'll light my own fucking candles. I'm done waiting, Aid. Done.

Before I can type a reply, she sends another text.

Kay-bear: Fuck. Said I'd ring my mother. I'll speak to you soon. Don't forget tomorrow night I'm out with Phillip if I don't get chance to text. xo

It was already happening. She hadn't even done more than have coffee with the guy and my contact with her was lessening. I needed to tell her how I felt, but only if things didn't work out with dickhead. Kaylie's happiness came before my own. Always had. Always would.

Her thirtieth was on Saturday and I hoped that he wouldn't be there that night by her side, because it was my place.

Mine.

11

KAYLIE

NOT WANTING to look like I've made too much of an effort, I drag on one of my trusty baggy outfits that Aiden hates and head out towards the restaurant. In true Phillip style, it's one he chose. He never was one to let me have my own mind, something I have plenty of these days, especially with the decision I finally made yesterday about my future possible pregnancy. So what if fate hasn't been on my side? If Phillip can't prove to me that he is actually serious about us having a second chance, then I'll be heading directly for the sperm bank very soon after my birthday. I will not hit thirty-one and not at least be pregnant.

"Reservation for Harrington?" I ask as I walk up towards the maître d'.

"You're the first. Follow me, please." I follow his lead, glancing around at all the couples enjoying themselves around the restaurant. "Can I get you a drink?"

"A chardonnay, please. A large one." I figure that if I've got to wait, I may as well enjoy myself.

The minutes tick by and my phone sits silently on the table as I drain my glass and pop the last olive I ordered into my mouth.

He's almost an hour late and he's not answering his phone.

I'm contemplating either ordering anyway seeing as I'm fucking starving or leaving and getting a greasy kebab on the way home, when an eruption of excitement comes from the corner of the restaurant. When I look over, there's a man down on one knee holding the hand of his shocked and sobbing girlfriend.

He says something to her which makes her cry harder before he slides a ring up her finger.

My stomach drops. Will that ever be me? Will I get my happily ever after or am I destined to spend the rest of my life alone with horrendous dates?

Deciding on spending the rest of the night alone with only a kebab to keep me company, I push the chair out behind me and reach to grab my bag from the floor.

"Kaykay, I'm so fucking sorry. I got caught on the phone with my father and then the fucking Tube just stopped between platforms. Just a fucking disaster. But I'm here now."

I should be glad he made it, right? I shouldn't be mourning the loss of my kebab I'd decided on.

"Ah good. I see you started without me." He nods towards my empty glass and little dish as he sits and grabs the menu waiting for him.

The waiter comes rushing over. He probably had a bet going with the others about how long I was prepared to wait.

"Can I get you a drink, sir?"

"Please could I have a glass of Châteauneuf-du-Pape."

"I'm sorry, sir. We only sell that by the bottle."

Phillip lets out a frustrated sigh before agreeing to a bottle and making a show of being seriously put out. "You'll have a glass with me." No question, just a demand. It's a harsh reminder of my old life.

"No, I don't like red."

"You used to."

I cringe at the reminder of what a pathetic cow I used to be. "No, Phillip, I've never liked it. I just used to play along to make you happy. I'm not that woman anymore. I've learnt there's more to life than making a man happy to your own detriment."

His mouth opens and closes, doing a great goldfish impression as he tries to figure out what to say.

"Well, I'm glad you made use of the past six years."

"What's that meant to mean?"

"You've clearly used the time to find yourself. That's admirable."

I snort in disbelief, my eyes threatening to pop out once again. "Is it?"

"I didn't mean it offensively."

"Good to know."

Thankfully, the waiter reappears with our drinks and makes a show of pouring a little of Phillip's pretentious wine choice into his glass. The pompous prick swirls it around before sniffing it and taking a sip to see if he approves. Of course, he may well have had a wine education since I last saw him, but I very much doubt it. This is all just a fucking show and all it achieves is to get my back up even more.

"Are you ready to order your food?" The waiter pulls his pad out of his apron after depositing his corkscrew.

"Yes, I'll have the fillet steak, rare of course. And she'll have the salmon."

"Excuse me? I'm more than capable of ordering my own dinner."

The waiter blushes as I stare daggers at Phillip. I wanted to believe that maybe he was right and he's changed over the past six years, but it seems like he's just as big a control freak as I remember.

"I'll also have the fillet steak, but medium-rare for me please."

Phillip waits for the waiter to be out of earshot before he speaks. "You don't like steak."

"No, I don't like red wine. I've always liked steak." It's a lie. I'm not really that keen but I remember him telling me that it's a man's meal and a lady should have something more delicate. Hence why I just ordered it. In reality, I'd have been more than happy with the salmon he wanted me to have, not that I'll ever admit that to him.

Phillip changes the subject to work and he chats about his first two days. I get to hear about each of his classes and his first impressions of every member of staff, none of which is too glowing. He always was a judgemental arsehole. I'm starting to question my younger self even more than I already was. I truly thought this guy was it for me.

The rest of the meal drags but thankfully they have an incredible chocolate fondant for dessert which perks things up a little.

"Shall we take this back to my place?" Phillip asks with a glint in his eye after he's paid the bill and escorts me out of the restaurant with his hand in the small of my back like he owns me.

"Um..." I stall, trying to come up with a decent excuse. "I promised my roommate I'd go home to help her with something."

"Can't you put her off until tomorrow night? It would be great for us to get properly reacquainted."

My stomach turns at the thought. I gave this guy my fucking virginity, that should be enough.

"I'm sorry. It has to be tonight. I'll see you at work tomorrow, yeah?"

Just at the perfect moment, a black cab drives around the corner and when I stick my hand out, he pulls over. I hop in before Phillip has a chance to stop me, and I tell the driver to step on it.

Walking in my flat, I'm greeted with silence. Kicking off my heels, I hang my coat and scarf on the hook by the front door.

Continuing down to my bedroom I shed my clothes in favour of my pyjamas. After getting myself a glass of water, I grab my laptop and tuck myself into bed. I try not to date on weeknights knowing I've got a room full of kids to deal with in the morning, but I made an exception tonight for Phillip knowing he'd also have the same prospect in the morning. I drink down half the water, wishing it was more wine. Anything to help wash away the memories of tonight.

I click on my bookmarks once my computer's powered up and find the sperm bank website I've looked at more times than I want to admit over the past few weeks.

Feeling brave after tonight's disaster, I pull up the contact page and send an enquiry. I told myself that if tonight went tits up that this was my next step and I don't intend on backing down now.

I'M on edge all day waiting for a response. Between that and not getting a reply when I messaged Aiden telling him what I'd done, I'm an anxious wreck. I know he's not happy about me even considering the sperm donor route but surely he's not so unhappy about it that he's going to ignore me. Is he?

It's just after lunch when distraction comes but it's really not the kind I'd ever wish for. My class is in the middle of silent reading time when screams filter down from one of the other classrooms swiftly followed by the fire alarm.

With my heart in my throat I try to calmly lead my kids out of the room and onto the assembly point out on the playground.

They might only be five and six but one look at the smoke pluming from the other end of the building and they go silent. They know as well as I do that this isn't a drill. I spy what looks like a child's face at the far window.

Knowing that I need to do something, I thrust the emergency register at my PA and go running into the building.

"Kaylie, what the hell are you doing?" she screams as I run as fast as my legs will carry me.

I know it's against all the rules but the thought of anyone in that classroom being stuck terrifies me enough to risk my own life. I'd give mine for a child's any day of the week.

The door handle is burning hot when I go to twist it, but seeing the flames inside, I use my cardigan to open it without burning myself.

I hesitate at the door for a few seconds, but the second I hear a scream I jump into action. Pulling the fabric up to cover my mouth and nose, I storm into the room to see if I can find anyone.

The smoke burns my eyes almost immediately, making it hard to see anything, but I don't stop. There are kids in here and I owe it to them to at least try to save them.

My lungs are burning, tears streaming down my face but eventually I find a group of five kids huddled in the corner shaking and screaming in fear.

"It's okay," I shout over the noise of the fire crackling behind us. "I've got you." My throat burns as I try to instruct them to get out, but a loud crack sounds out before a thunderous crash makes us all squeal. Part of the ceiling caves in, blocking our way out and it's the first time I allow any real panic to settle in me. Adrenaline got me this far but seeing as I've now got nowhere to turn, I start to freak out. My chest heaves as I try to drag in any oxygen left in the room as the five kids cling to me for dear life.

"It'll be okay. They'll rescue us. We'll be fine," I say, though I don't know if it's the truth.

12

AIDEN

I'M ENJOYING a bacon sandwich when the call comes in. Fire at Kaylie's school. My heart thumps in my chest so bad I think it's going to come up and out of my throat. I have to forget she could be there right now, it's time to focus my mind on the procedures. One mistake can cost one of my fire family member's lives.

We're on our way, sirens blazing. More information comes in that it's a classroom and part of a roof has collapsed. Children and a teacher are trapped inside. I don't even wish it was Phillip. There are kids trapped. This cannot be a day where kids die, it can't.

We're on scene and tackling the blaze and I see him. Dickhead. To be fair he does look pale and worried, but I can't see Kaylie. I cannot fucking see Kaylie. But again, it doesn't matter who is behind that door right now. Just that we get them out.

"Let's do this." Our gaffer shouts and we're shouting for people to keep clear of the door and we're breaking it down...

There's so much smoke but we can see that Kaylie is on the floor with five kids, keeping them low. She has them next to a vent. Their skin is black and I can tell they're all struggling. Then we have masks on them and they're being carried out.

I wrap Kaylie in my arms, thankful that she's alive and as I think that, she falls unconscious.

She's placed in an ambulance but I can't go with her. I've called her mother and told her where she's headed. Now I have to make sure the fire is securely out and then I'll be asking my boss if I can go straight to the hospital.

Once the area is completely secure, we start to do our origin investigation. "It looks like it started in the stockroom. Go and speak to whoever's classroom it is, see if they can shed any light on it, Aiden."

I reach outside and pull off my helmet. A middle-aged woman comes running over to me, introducing herself as the headteacher. "Can you tell me whose classroom it is please, ma'am. I need to ask them some questions." I say, interrupting her own conversation.

"Of course. Of course. Mr Harrington. Could you come over?"

Fuck my life. It's dipshit's classroom.

He walks over in the haughty manner I remember. "Do I know you?" he says. "You look familiar."

"If you could just answer some questions for me please, sir. I understand it's your classroom. Do you have any idea what could have started the blaze?"

"No. I'm afraid not. I smelled burning and got the children out of the classroom and sounded the fire alarm. I don't know how the other children got in there. Miss Hale was outside with me and made the foolish decision to run back in the building instead of waiting for you to arrive."

I want to kill him with my bare hands. Except they're currently covered in gloves.

"Excuse me." I turn to face a teacher holding a child's hand. The kid looks around eleven years old.

"Yes?" I ask.

"Could we have a word in private please, about the fire?"

"Sure. Excuse me a moment." I say to the headmistress and fucktard.

"This is William. He was in the classroom this morning. He said that it was supposed to be maths, but the teacher said that this morning they could have a free period and go on the computers. William says that Mr Harrington went out of the classroom for a considerable period of time and Coby Everett and Kenzie Smyth went into the stock room because they'd found some cigarettes and a packet of matches."

"Carry on."

"Will I get into trouble for telling you?" William's lip wobbles.

"Not at all. Scout's honour. Tell you what. How about a look around the station sometime? Bring some friends. You can go on the appliances."

He nods his head vigorously.

"They got the matches and cigarettes from the floor near Mr Harrington's chair. He was gone ages. When he came back, they'd started the fire. He smelled burning and told us all to get out and he tried to count us but I kept telling him we weren't all there. Some of the girls were frightened and had hidden behind the curtain. He wouldn't listen."

"You are a very brave boy for trying to rescue your classmates and I'll be recommending you for an award, young man. Now let your teacher take you back to where children are meeting their parents." I nodded to the teacher with him. Then as soon as they've left, I walk over to the police officers on scene.

I watch as they approach Phillip. Watch him check his pockets. Watch the realisation dawn. What a fucking idiot.

But I have no more time for him. Back at the station I change as quickly as I can and then I'm off to the hospital, hoping that Kaylie is going to be okay.

I find Kaylie's brother Jenson in the waiting room and envelope him in my arms.

"Fuck, man. Mum says you brought her out of the building. I can't thank you enough."

When I look he's in tears.

"How is she?"

"Doing okay. They need to assess her for twenty-four hours for the smoke inhalation. But her sputum was clear and whatever other tests they banged on about. Said she'll have a cough for a day or two, but if all goes okay she'll be out tomorrow afternoon."

"Your parents in with her?"

He nodded. "Yeah. Go on through. I'd better update Leah. She'll be going demented and it'll not be good for the baby."

I walk over to the room she's currently in and wave from the doorway.

"Aiden. Oh my god, Aiden. You're our hero. You saved our girl." Kaylie's mum flies at me and then her dad shakes my hand and gives me a man hug.

"Just doing my job, but of course, it was Kaylie. Can't have anything happening to my girl."

Kaylie is awake but has an oxygen mask on. She takes it off to say something but starts coughing.

"Put that back on right now, young lady. For goodness' sake, you can thank Aiden later," her mum snaps at her following it up with a gentle stroke down her cheek and a rearrange of the mask to ensure it's fitting properly. Kaylie rolls her eyes at me and I smirk.

"Thank God you're alive and will be out in plenty of time for that party. I know being thirty is a milestone for you but trying to top yourself was a bit extreme."

Her eyes narrow as she knows she can't give me a sassy retort.

"Do they know how it happened?" her dad asks me.

"They have their suspicions, but they have to confirm it. Seems to have started in the stock room."

Again those eyes are staring at me but I'm not

going to say anything further. Not while she's being monitored. I can't be having her getting worked up.

"Well, I just wanted to check she was okay. I'll head off home now. It's been a long day and I could use another shower."

"Would you stay five minutes just while we go get some drinks and sandwiches? Or until Jenson comes back?"

"Of course I will," I reply. They leave the room and leave me alone with Kaylie. A captive audience.

"I'm not going to tell you off for running into that classroom even though it was against all procedures. Because you kept those kids safe and calm while they must have been going out of their minds. You're the hero, Miss Kaylie Hale, not me. I'm just the firefighter who broke down the door and carried the hero out."

She can't help it, she lifts the oxygen mask off again and croaks, "both heroes," before putting it back in place.

"I'm so fucking glad you're alive. Don't ever do this to me again. Promise?"

She nods. She's looking tired, fighting to keep her eyes open. I hear her parents' voices approaching, getting nearer.

Standing by her bed, I lift her oxygen mask and

put my lips on hers, briefly. Just a brush of my lips against her own.

I stand back to see her reaction but she's asleep. I've no idea if she knows I did it or not. All I know is I want to kiss her over and over again.

KAYLIE IS DISCHARGED the next day. Her mother wants her home with her but after protests with lots of coughing I agree that I will stay with her. This satisfies both Kaylie and her mother as Mrs Hale is satisfied that she's under the best possible care with me being a fireman and Kaylie is satisfied that she's away from her overprotective mother.

"Thank fuck," she says when we get back to her flat. I look around and note half the furniture is missing from the place. There's no sofa or television.

"What the fuck?"

"She moved out. Cheryl moved out. She said she was going but obviously my being in hospital was the perfect time for her to escape. One month's rent and then I have to look at moving. Right at bloody Christmas." She starts coughing again.

"I'm getting you some water. Calm down, we'll sort something. Now, while you're recuperating is not the time to be getting stressed." I steer her towards her bedroom. "Go and get into your pyjamas while I get you some water."

Heading back into her bedroom I remember that she only has a single bed. "Hutch up, looks like we're getting cosy tonight." I climb on the bed beside her handing her the drink. She takes a few sips of water and places it on her bedside table and passes me the remote.

"Here, find us something to watch," she says settling back against the pillows.

Tomorrow I will tell her about Phillip. That he won't be welcome back at her or any school any time soon. I don't know how she left things with him after their date. I don't know how she'll respond, but I do know I need to tell her how I feel soon. Knowing how fast I could have lost her. That she could have perished in that fire. It shows me that I'm going to have to confess everything. She must not have been awake when I kissed her because she's never mentioned it and I'm sure she would have done, even if just to ask me what the fuck I was playing at.

And if she doesn't want me romantically? Well, I'm going to offer to be her sperm donor. But I'll do it the way she wants it, soft music and candlelight. The old-fashioned way. So tomorrow, I'll talk to her about

Phillip, and then I'll let her process that and recover ready for her party. But after her party, then we need to talk.

I'm so fucking nervous.

"You going to find a programme or spend the night in a dreamworld?"

"Sorry."

I flick through the channels and find an Avengers film partway through. Lots of man totty for her and Scarlett Johansson for me.

"Do you want something to eat?"

"No thanks. I've already been rescued from one fire this week, don't want you burning down the kitchen. That's if Cheryl left the cooker."

"We'll get all that sorted after your birthday. I promise. Cheryl is not ruining your celebrations okay?"

"Okay. Now can you be quiet because Loki's just come on screen."

I want to say I'm better than Tom Hiddleston but Kaylie looks content and comfortable, so I just snuggle in closer and watch the film until she falls asleep, her head on my arm.

13
───────

KAYLIE

I WAKE to the driest sore throat and pounding head I think I've ever experienced, but neither is the most insistent feeling in my body. That comes courtesy of the low throb coming from between my legs and it doesn't take my sleep fogged brain long to realise why.

I'm not alone in this bed and my companion is curled around me like a freaking snake.

My heart rate increases as realisation dawns. His arm isn't just wrapped around me. It's also under my tank with his hand cupping my breast.

Fuck.

I try to ease away from him, but all it achieves is for his grip to tighten.

"Kaylie," he breathes, his voice desperate and

needy. Then he does something that really freaks me out, he moves his hips slightly and the unmistakable feeling of his solid length pressing into my arse makes me gasp. "Kaylie, mmmm..." he moans. He'd better not be having a fucking sex dream about me.

My heart thunders in my chest but I don't panic as much as I thought I might in this situation.

As I lay there trying to figure out how I feel right now, a memory hits me.

I was lying in that hospital bed. Aiden was sitting beside me about to say goodbye. But before he left, he lifted my mask and brushed his lips against mine.

That was a dream, right? That didn't actually happen? Imagining him doing that was just my imagination after he rescued me. He saved my life and that along with the smoke inhalation screwed with my brain, right?

My mind spins as I try to come up with reasons as to why that didn't really happen when Aiden's fingers move against my nipple. It puckers under his touch sending a bolt of electricity to shoot towards my sex.

"Fuck. Shit." I jump from the bed in panic, totally freaked out by my reaction to his touch.

My body doesn't know it's him. It's just reacting to touch. It's natural. I tell myself as I back away.

"What's wrong?" His sleepy, rough voice fills my ears and I lift my eyes from the floor.

"I... uh..." His long, lean body is stretched out on my bed, pressed right up against the wall in only a tiny pair of boxer briefs. Inches of perfection greet me before the most obvious bulge catches my eye. The insistent throb between my legs kicks up a notch as I fight to drag my eyes away.

I shouldn't be looking at my best friend like this. *But you're that desperate,* a little voice in my head screams. *Just think how good he could make you feel.*

"No," I shout, making Aiden jump.

"What? I didn't ask you anything.

"Cover that up, Aid. I need coffee before dealing with you exposing yourself."

He glances down his body. "Shit." Dragging the covers over his bottom half, he doesn't look half as embarrassed as he should.

I'm still staring, I know I am but my mind's racing at a million miles a minute with thoughts that should not be allowed in my head. My chest heaves as I try to fight the unwanted desire that's still raging within me.

I really need to find someone willing to shag me to put me out of my misery.

"Kaylie, are you okay?"

His eyes drop to my chest and it's only then I realise that my nipples are trying to fight their way through the fabric of my tank.

"Fuck. I need... I need to..." Spinning on my heels, I march from the room and slam the newly fitted bathroom door when I get there.

Dropping down onto the toilet, I go about my business before sitting back, the events of the past few minutes running on repeat in my mind.

"What were you thinking?" I ask myself, slapping my palm against my forehead. "So not appropriate. I know I just had a near death experience but there's no need to go all crazy."

"Are you talking to yourself in there?" Aiden calls out.

"Fuck. I'll be out in a minute."

When I do open the door, it's no more than to crack it open enough to see if he's in view. I breathe a sigh of relief when he's not and run for my bedroom, grabbing an oversized hoodie and pulling it over my head to cover up.

The scent of fresh coffee hits my nose and my mouth waters. With one last glance at where he was laid almost naked not so long ago, I sigh and walk towards the kitchen.

I keep my gaze down, not knowing how he's going to react to what happened this morning.

"How are you feeling?" he asks, placing a mug down in front of me.

"Oh... um..." I panic, my body temperature soaring, making me regret the hoodie. "Well, I wasn't expecting—"

"I meant your head and throat."

"Oh... yeah, better thank you. This will help too, I'm sure."

Glancing up at him, I find he's now fully dressed in yesterday's clothes. I'm not sure if I'm relieved or disappointed.

I'm desperately trying to come up with something to say to distract myself from the image of him on my bed that seems to be burned into my fucking eyelids when he speaks.

"I need to tell you something."

"Oh?"

He shifts uncomfortably in his seat and my pulse picks up in anticipation. Is he about to tell me that he did kiss me and that he wants to do it again? Or that he knew where his hand was this morning?

"It's about the fire." Those four words sure put out the fire that was about to rage inside of me. "We know how it started."

"Why do you look so nervous to tell me? Fuck, was it my fault?" I've no idea how it could be seeing as it was at the other end of the school but the way he's looking at me with deep creases in his forehead leads me to think crazy things. Concern isn't a look I see on Aiden often so when it's there I know it's serious.

"No, no, of course not. It was Phillip's."

"What?" My brows pull together in confusion.

"He left the room. A couple of kids found his fags and lighter and took them to the stock room to play with. The next thing everyone knew the place was alight."

"Fuck. What's going to happen to him?" My voice comes out sounding much more concerned than I really am. I'd pretty much come to the conclusion the universe hadn't brought him back to my life for any good reason.

"Pretty sure you won't be seeing him at your school again, that's for sure. His neglect almost resulted in the death of five kids and another teacher." His face pales as he thinks back. "I doubt he'll be welcome in many schools after that."

"Jesus," I mutter, wondering how you even begin to deal with that.

"Couldn't have happened to a nicer bloke if you ask me."

"That's enough. I've not got the energy for Phillip bashing right now."

"Are you sure you're feeling okay? I've got a shift in a bit, but I can see if someone will swap."

"No, no, I'm good. You can go." I try not to put too much emphasis on the idea of him leaving, but after this morning, I really need an Aiden free space.

He hesitates after putting his empty mug in the sink.

"I'm on a late shift. Do you want me to come here after to check on you?"

The thought of having a repeat of this morning is enough to have me shouting "No!" in a panic.

"Okaaay. Can I call once I'm home just so I know you're okay?"

"I'll text you if I go to bed before you ring."

"Promise me you'll call me if you start feeling ill. I hate the idea of you being alone and suffering."

"Aiden, I'm fine. You heard the doctors."

"I know." He looks like he wants to say more but he keeps his lips sealed.

Saying goodbye to him is awkward in a way I've never experienced with him before and I don't like it. I've never had anything like this morning with Aiden before, ever. So the fact he caused that kind of reaction within me is enough to knock me off kilter more than a little.

———

BY LATE AFTERNOON I'm going stir crazy. I hate sitting around the house knowing I should be relaxing. It's just like telling someone they can't push the big red button.

I get so fed up with myself that in the end I pull my coat and scarf on and head out. My birthday party is tomorrow night and I have nothing to wear that's worthy of a thirtieth.

I take it slow as I head towards Oxford Street. The fresh air invigorates me as much as it makes me cough so I keep going.

I try on dress after dress trying to find something that is equal parts a cover up and sexy. It's easier said than done. They either expose way too much boob or much too much thigh.

I must have tried on at least twenty before I find what I think is the one.

Twirling around in the mirror I take in the sequined halter neck which is cut low enough to give a hint of what I'm hiding beneath and then the flowing skirt that kicks out from around my waist and hangs just a little above my knee. What I really love though is that the black dress has a red lining that can only be seen when the skirt swishes. It is a perfect statement dress and something that I don't think any of my friends and family will expect. Even more reason to drop more money than I've ever spent on a dress before. My birthday tomorrow marks another chapter in my life. One where I'm going to have what I've always wanted. A baby. It might not happen the conventional way, but I don't care. I need to do this for me.

I manage to find a killer pair of red shoes to go with my dress and a matching red clutch. When I walk out of the shop with my bags swinging from my fingers, I feel much more like myself than I have in ages despite the cough that keeps catching me off guard. For the first time in a long time, I've got a plan. A plan that is going to get me exactly what I want and put paid to my previous plan of finding Mr Right. Maybe I'm not destined to ever find him, and do you know what? I'm totally fine with that. I don't need a man. I am more than capable of being in charge of my own destiny.

I get back to my house late with my new purchases and cartons of my favourite Chinese takeaway which I take to bed with me to indulge in. Turning the TV on, I find Bridget Jones' diary has just started. I smile to myself and stuff some noodles into my mouth.

"We've got this, Bridge. We've got this."

14

AIDEN

WHO INVENTED SINGLE BEDS? Bastards. I had my chubby sticking in her but not in the right place. I had to think about Brandon naked to make it go down and then I basically ran to the kitchen after getting dressed.

Kaylie seemed okay. Just needs some more time to recover, so I'll leave her alone until her party now. Which reminds me, I need to get her a present. It's a special birthday. For mine she got me Formula One tickets. What the hell can I buy her? A massive box of Godiva chocolate is a given, but I'll have to ponder anything else after my shift.

I nip to the Godiva shop on the way home. There's nothing like cutting it fine. I ask for a hamper around the £100 mark. It's in a gift box so that's fantastic, no wrapping. Then I pop to another store and get her a chocolate fondue set because I don't think she's ever bought one. I've not spent anywhere near enough or got anything special enough. I walk into a jewellery shop and the woman behind the counter obviously sees a desperate expression because she beckons me over after watching me wandering and sighing for five minutes.

"I need a present for my best friend."

"Okay, so what about a watch? We do some great guy's gifts."

"Oh no." I shake my head. "My best friend is a woman. I've known her since we were six and now she's thirty."

"Riggghhtt, erm so tell me a little about her, so I can get an idea of her likes and dislikes."

"She loves chocolate. Hates apples. She's single. She wants to be a mum."

"I was thinking more favourite colours."

"Oh. Well, erm, red. She likes red."

I leave with a ruby pendant for her and some matching earrings and once again a gift box comes to the rescue. Job done. Now all I have to do is get a card. A jokey 29-forever card does the trick and I'm off home. Tomorrow morning, I shall make my way round to her flat with a birthday breakfast as is our tradition and then I'll leave her to get ready for the party and go home and shit myself while I try to get the guts up to confess my feelings. I'll tell her Sunday for definite. It could spoil her birthday if it all went wrong. Sunday it is.

———

I CAN'T SLEEP, so at nine am, after sneaking through the entrance with another resident, I'm banging on the door of Kaylie's flat armed with her presents and birthday breakfast stuff.

She eventually opens the door, bleary-eyed and her hair stuck up at all angles. "Happy birthday to you, happy birthday to you, happy birthday dear Kay-bear. Happy birthday to youuuuuuu." I serenade.

She shuts the door in my face.

What?

A minute later she opens it again standing armed with a water pistol I brought around once for a laugh.

"You sing like that again and you get it."

"Look, I'm a beautiful guy and a firefighter hero. I can't be greedy and be able to sing too. I have to give other guys a chance. Now are you going to let me in, or do I have to go knock on the doors of the other residents looking for a hot woman who'd like all these gifts and my company for breakfast?"

"Please stop or I'll not want to eat anything for puking."

Once inside, she hits the shower while I go to the kitchen and fix her buck's fizz and a cooked breakfast.

I'd not realised how hungry I was myself and once she appears we tuck in heartily to the food.

"I'll need to line my stomach for tonight. I need to drink just to survive my family. My mother is still panicking I'm going to get a collapsed lung."

I laugh.

"You can laugh. She loves you. She's now asking why we've never got together. I told her to ask you."

"You didn't?!"

"I bloody did. I have to put up with the collapsed lung grief so you can deal with the why we aren't romantically involved questions."

"I think I'm starting to feel a bit ill. Might not make it."

"If I can make it after surviving a fire, you can come stand in the path of the mother inferno. Just start snogging another guest or something. That'll shut her up."

I will need to put her mother off the scent. I don't

want her having any hint of what I'm intending to say to Kaylie on Sunday. There's bound to be someone there I can flirt with.

"Present time!" I declare, changing the subject.

I give her the chocolates and she opens them and looks at me strangely.

"Erm. Thank you." She puts the hamper down on the side looking uncomfortable. It's no good, I'm a nosy bastard, so I look to see why she's not jumping up and down in chocolate lover joy.

Godiva Carnival of Passion and Fun Hamper.

What in God's name?

Luckily it is full of chocolate and doesn't contain a dildo or a pair of handcuffs.

"Oh bloody hell. I just picked it up quick yesterday. I didn't see the name."

Her eyes narrow.

"You spent a lot of time considering what to buy me then?"

"Here just open the next one." I pass her the next box and she unwraps the chocolate fondue set. Once again there's an unexpected expression on her face. Is this... disappointment?

"I know how much you love chocolate, so I thought about this present for a while, so see I did consider what to buy you." I try and big up my gift that for some reason isn't hitting the mark.

She walks over to her kitchen cupboards and chooses the one in the furthest corner and she swings open the cupboard door. Behind is a chocolate fondue set.

"You bought me that five years ago for Christmas."

Fuck. Did I? In all honesty I probably got my mother to get me a present and wrap it up.

"It's that hammer attack to my eye. It's damaged part of my brain. I'm going to have to see a doctor about my new memory problems."

She gives me evil side-eye.

"Anyway, they were just bits of something. This is your main present." I hand her the jewellery bag and she opens it looking like she's expecting me to have wrapped a turd. Then her entire expression softens as she opens the first box and sees the pendant.

"They're rubies. Not any fake stones," I add.

"Oh my god, it's beautiful." She opens the box with the earrings next. "Aiden, these will look amazing with my party dress. Oh my. They're so beautiful."

Looks like the other presents are forgotten and

I'm forgiven as she jumps up and over to me and hugs me. Her soft tits press against me and my dick swells.

"So how's turning thirty then?" I say through a mouthful of Kaylie flesh.

"If I'm going to get jewellery, not so bad." She goes back to her seat. "Thank you for being here on my birthday morning, Aid. Everyone else was just 'see you at the party'. It would be boring without you here."

Yep, and that is want I want you to realise. That without me your life's boring and unfulfilled.

The doorbell rings. *Thank fuck.* I think, they said they'd deliver before lunch. Kaylie goes to the door and I follow behind her. Sure enough it's the furniture delivery company with a brand new double bed and mattress for Kaylie.

"Surprise." I tell her. It was an afterthought last night and so I rang the local furniture store this morning and begged and bribed them to come out with an ex-display model.

After it's put in place (the old one shoved in Cheryl's old room for now), we spend the rest of the morning drinking coffee and chatting about nothing in particular and then I leave her because she wants to go and buy new double bedding and get ready for the party. I'm picking her up at seven so she can get there in plenty of time.

BEFORE LONG I'M back in a car heading towards her place once more. But I'm not in my own car. I've hired a limo with champagne and I'm sitting in the back. She'll be making her way to InHale in style. Knocking on her door, I'm blown away by the vision that answers. Her hair is in these curls that I want to wrap my fist around. Her eyes look huge and doe-like because her make-up is accentuating her natural beauty. The dress she has gives a taste of those breasts. She gives me a twirl and the skirt of the dress swishes revealing a flash of red, and shapely thighs. I'm gonna have blue balls.

"You look amazing. Your carriage awaits." I gesture behind me.

"Really? A limo. Wow. You spoil me." A huge grin lights up her features. I hold out a hand to her and she takes it as she leaves the flat. She drops my hand to lock up and I feel sad. Jesus, I think I grew a vagina. She turns back to me and the ruby pendant sparkles under the streetlight. I reach out and lift it. It rests just above the swell of her breasts and my fingers touch her skin as I take the pendant in my hand.

"It's beautiful, like the woman wearing it."

A moment passes between us, a beat, where it could be my imagination but I'm sure there's a connection.

Then the fucking limo driver gets out and opens the car door, shouting "Happy birthday, Madam, your ride awaits."

Wrong fucking ride, mate. It's my dick I want her to ride right now.

She loops her arm through mine and we walk down the path to the car together and climb inside. Then we're on our way, via a scenic route, while we drink champagne.

"Are you prepared for my mother?"

"Yeah, I'm gonna ask if she's bored with your dad yet."

"Might want to rethink that cos I think she'd ditch him and ask where to sign up."

"I'll just have to shamelessly flirt with someone else then." I hint at her. The thick cow doesn't get it. Instead her expression clouds a little.

"Yeah, use my party as a pussy party. Bound to be someone there for you to tap."

"That's not what I meant." I'm about to start

explaining when we arrive and of course everyone is outside waiting for the birthday girl.

We exit the limo and she's enveloped in family and friends and whisked into the restaurant's private party room while I stand frustrated in more ways than one.

I greet the people I know and stand with Jenson and Leah. It's adults only so their daughter Amelia is with a sitter.

"Oh yeah, how did that go down when you told her?" I ask them. Amelia is a recently seven-year-old, spitfire.

"She told her father he was a basic bitch." Leah raises a brow. I fall about laughing. "How come kids weren't allowed anyway? I know there's alcohol but..."

Leah points toward the door where a ripped and toned male body is coming through carrying a tray of drinks. The only thing he's wearing is an apron. His muscled arse dimples as he walks towards Kaylie.

Everyone's eyes are on him as he basically prowls towards her. This man is cocksure, confident, charismatic. I can see all the women swooning, except one. The waitress dressed in normal wait clothes. She's sneering at him. Fucking Scott. How come tonight he's not working downstairs and is instead on naked waiter duty?

"Whose idea was that?" I snap.

Leah looks at me, studying my face a little too long. "Mine. She's not had any naked arse in her life for a while. I thought it was time."

"She shouldn't be anywhere near that manwhore."

Jenson is talking to someone else now, Leah moves closer to me. "For a best friend you sure seem a little put out about Scott. Is that because you're jealous?"

"No, of course not," I bluster. "I think it's a great idea. I'm actually thinking of cracking on with the waitress."

"Really?" Leah looks bemused. "Suki's lovely. Feisty though."

"Just as I like 'em."

Leah sighs. "Sometimes you men are such dickheads." She walks away from me, back to her husband.

I watch seething as one dickhead, his arse hanging out, flirts shamelessly with Kaylie, and what does she do? She laps it right up.

Fuck this. I head in the direction of the sneery-faced waitress. Two can play at that game.

15

KAYLIE

I'VE no intention of telling Leah, but this whole 'butler in the buff' is so not my thing. I feel slightly more comfortable knowing it's Scott and that he's probably under strict instructions from my big brother not to lay a finger on me.

I was too distracted by said waiter along with all my other friends and family to notice what happened to Aiden, but I soon find him when we're instructed to take our seats. He's leaning over the bar whispering something in Suki, the bartenders, ear.

The way she's smiling at him causes something I don't like to stir in my belly. She's not really his type so I figure I'm just being protective.

"Hey, did you hear? They're about to bring our starters."

"Oh, right. I'll be over in a few. I'm a little busy right now." Aiden barely manages to drag his eyes away from Suki to even bother looking at me. Glancing at her, I watch as her eyes hold his, pure sex appeal oozing from them in a way I could only dream of.

"Great, knock yourself out." I don't mean to snap, but whatever was in my belly moments ago is starting to spread throughout my entire body.

I want Aiden's attention tonight. The way he looked at me when I first opened the door. His eyes darkened and the muscles in his neck rippled as he swallowed. I don't think I've ever felt as beautiful. And when he reached out for my necklace, I swear he was going for my face like he wanted to kiss me. I only just about stopped myself from leaning in.

What the fuck is wrong with me?

I can't help but look back over my shoulder at them when I get to my seat. The space beside my chair is empty, waiting for the idiot at the bar. When I find them, they're both staring right at me with smiles on their faces.

I feel ridiculous, but knowing they're laughing at me, tonight of all nights, has tears begging to flow and a lump in my throat.

I don't want to watch my best friend pull tonight. I want him all to myself.

Shit.

The realisation hits me like a fucking articulated lorry.

Everyone chats around me as I lose myself in my panicked thoughts. Do I want him, want him? Or is it just in an 'I'm still single on my thirtieth birthday' kind of way and know he'll be able to finish the day off right?

Fuck. This is a disaster.

It must be the champagne.

The fancy pants starter that Jenson came up with consisting of smoked salmon and some funky looking green stuff is placed in front of me but after starving myself after breakfast in preparation, I'm suddenly not at all hungry. Well, not for food.

I risk a glance towards Aiden to find out if he's fucking her against the bar yet, to find him walking my way. His eyes are locked on me as he drops into his chair.

"Hey, beautiful. You enjoying yourself?"

Watching you eye fuck the staff, yeah great. I manage to keep that as an internal thought and instead, smile sweetly and say, "Sure am. Scott was certainly a nice surprise. It's the closest thing I've had to sex in a very long time."

"Now, Kay-bear, that's not true, and you know it."

"Do I? Please correct me if I'm wrong but I'm pretty sure no cock has been anywhere near my body."

He leans in. His manly scent fills my nose and the scruff on his cheeks tickles against mine. "I'm pretty sure you woke up *very* close to a cock the other morning. *And* I'm pretty sure you liked it."

Holy fucking... My cheeks heat as memories of his body wrapped around mine fill my mind. I squeeze my thighs together as I remember how it felt with his hot palm cupping my naked breast.

"I... uh..." Aiden pulls back, his eyes bounce between mine and his starter as he awaits my response but as if he knows I need rescuing, Scott steps between us filling my gaze with hard muscle and bronzed skin.

"Refill, princess?"

"Yes, yes please." My voice is rough even to my own ears.

"A few more of these down you and we should have a good night on our hands. You know you want to see what I'm hiding under this apron." Scott winks at me, slightly turning up the edge of the fabric, before moving down the table to flirt with my mother. *Cringe.*

When I look back to Aiden, his eyes are narrowed at me and his lips are pressed into a hard line.

"What? Jealous?"

"Of his body? Not at all. Mine's better."

"Riiight." I roll my eyes at his one-sided pissing contest with Scott.

Turning away from him, I pick up my fork and dig into my starter.

Aiden's stare doesn't leave me. It burns into the side of my face making me nervous about eating while under such harsh scrutiny.

I've just taken a bite when he leans in once again. "I'll let you compare later if you'd like? I think it's important it's a fair competition."

The taste of the incredible food explodes on my tongue at the exact time he whispers in my ear and I moan in delight... *for the food. It's definitely for the food.*

He sits back and sets about eating his own starter, but the only thing I can focus on are his words.

He is jealous.

The rest of the night continues in a similar fashion. Scott's flirtation gets more and more inappropriate and Aiden's death stares get more and more threatening. But that doesn't stop him making a play for Suki, mind you.

"He wants you so fucking bad, princess. I'm pretty sure his balls might explode if you don't let him bang you tonight."

"I'm sorry what?" I splutter when Scott comes back once again to refill my glass.

"Aiden," he says, jutting his chin out in his direction. "He wants you... baaad."

"Are you blind? He's spent almost all night giving Suki his come-to-bed-with-me eyes."

"Princess, you're not dumb so please don't act like you are. He wants you and he's using Suki to make a point. He wants her about as much as he does me." He leaves me with that final nugget of information and continues around the room with his bottle, clenching his arse muscles every time a woman so much as glances in his direction.

Scott's words are on repeat for the rest of the party. My head spins as I say goodbye to everyone who got dressed up and came out tonight to help me celebrate and soon it's just Jenson, Leah, Aiden and me left. Well, Aiden's not really with us because he's still at the fucking bar making Suki throw her head back in laughter.

"Any plans for the rest of the night?" Leah asks.

"I don't think so. Just heading home."

"Jesus, Kay. You're thirty, not seventy. You can still go out and enjoy yourself, you know?" Jenson says with a roll of his eyes.

Leah slaps him on the shoulder. "If Kaylie just wants to go home, then that's up to her."

Jenson scoffs but heads off towards the kitchen when Scott beckons him.

"You going home with Aiden?"

"What? No, of course not. He's my best friend," I snap.

"Whoa." Leah puts her hands up in defence. "I meant in a taxi. I wasn't suggesting you were going to... wait," she sings as her eyes widen in delight. "You do want to *go home* with him, don't you?"

"Don't be silly. This is Aiden we're talking about, total manwhore. I wouldn't touch him with—"

"Hey, you ready to make a move?"

My cheeks flame bright red as my temperature soars. Please tell me he didn't just hear that.

"Uh... yeah. I'm ready. I just need to..." I rush over to the table that's littered with presents and start collecting everything up.

I know Leah and Aiden are staring at me. Tingles are running up and down my spine, but I refuse to turn around.

Eventually though, I don't have much choice.

"Here, let me take those." Aiden reaches out to take the box from my hands, but instead of grabbing onto the box, his hands cover mine. Something shoots up both my arms and our eyes connect. He felt it too. Something passes between us, just like it did out the front of my building when he first picked me up.

"Th- thank you," I stutter, feeling all out of sorts.

"Anything for you."

My breath catches at the honesty in his tone. It's not the first time he's ever said something like that, but it feels like the first time he's really meant it.

"Go on, get out of here, you two, so my guys can clean up," Jenson calls.

"Oh, yeah. Sure." Dragging my eyes away from Aiden's grey ones, I look up to my brother.

"Thank you so much for tonight. Everything was incredible; even if I had to look at Scott's arse all night."

"You loved it," is shouted from somewhere making Jenson shake his head in frustration.

"You're welcome. I'm glad you had a good night.

Now, off you go and make the most of that limo Aiden paid a fortune for."

"We've still got it?" I turn back to Aiden who's staring intently at me, an unreadable expression on his face.

"Yeah, I booked it for the whole night."

"Sweet. Let's go and have a little party for two in the back then. Grab another bottle of bubbles, I'm sure he won't notice."

"I have to pay for that you know?" Jenson grumbles behind me.

"Oh shush, you can afford it."

Leah appears with a bottle and shoves it under Aiden's arm before we make our way out with all my gifts.

The limo is idling at the curb, helping to make InHale look even more exclusive than it already does.

We get everything loaded up before climbing in and pouring glasses of champagne.

I'm on my second glass, the alcohol is nicely buzzing around my system and I have no idea where we are seeing as Aiden told the driver to just drive.

"You know, I've always wanted to have sex in a limo. I read it in a book a few years ago. Man, it was hot."

Aiden clears his throat. "Is that right?"

"Yeah. Maybe I should have invited Scott to join me instead? He could have fulfilled that little fantasy as a birthday present to me. He was dressed ready for it."

Aiden growls like a fucking wild animal, making me do a double take at him. His eyes are equally as wild as the muscle in his neck thumps showing how frustrated he is right now.

"What is it you think he can do that I can't?"

"Uh..."

Pushing himself from the seat he was relaxing back in, he drops to his knees in front of me and plucks the glass from my hand.

"You want something. You fucking ask me. You got that?"

"Um..."

Before I register what's happening, his hands are cupping my cheeks and his forehead is pressed against mine. His chest heaves as his champagne scented breath races past my lips.

"Tell me you don't feel it?"

My lips part, but no words find their way out.

"Kay-bear, you need to tell me right now if you don't want this because I can't wait any fucking longer to kiss you again."

To kiss me again? So he did kiss me in the hospital.

I don't get a chance to respond because he either takes my silence as confirmation that I do want it or his restraint snaps, because his hands tilt my head to the side and his lips slam down on mine.

Fuck.

16

AIDEN

I'M DONE WAITING.

My lips slam down on hers, claiming hers in a bruising kiss. It's like passion and punishment combined. My feelings for her pouring into the moment while I want to wipe out any passing thoughts she may have about Scott, my frustration at their stupid flirting all night.

I break off and sit back on my knees, my breath coming in hard gasps. Kaylie places her fingertips against her lips.

"I'm asking you one more time. Do you want me? Not as a best friend, Kaylie. Do. You. Want. Me?"

"Yes." Escapes her mouth and it's the sweetest sound I ever heard.

I press the intercom to talk to the driver. "We're ready to be driven home now thanks."

Her eyes flash with lust and I sit down next to her and pull her close to me. I want to fuck her on the back seat of this limo, but I won't. That's what the new bed is for.

"I thought you were into Suki," she says softly. There's a vulnerability to the sound. I don't like that I put it there.

"I was just trying to make you jealous for eye-fucking Scott."

She bursts into noisy laughter. "I was trying to make you jealous too."

I scrub a hand through my hair. "We're fucking idiots."

Sliding my hand up the back of her neck, I twist my fingers in her curled hair and pull her back to me. My lips brush hers gently a couple of times, just in case she's going to change her mind. It's her last chance because once this starts I know I'm not going to be able to stop.

Her confirmation comes courtesy of a soft whimper and my restraint snaps. I press harder against her lips and slide my tongue between them, seeking hers out. Her unique sweet taste mixes with the champagne we've been drinking and it sends me higher than any fucking drug could. This has been a long time coming and I intend on getting as much of her as I can.

With her pressed up against my side, one hand in her hair and the other resting on her waist, just itching to explore, I kiss her the rest of the way home.

Being polite to the limo driver is excruciating. The minute he is gone, I wait for Kaylie to buzz us through her building and then we take to the stairs, neither of us having the patience to wait for the lift. She opens the door to her flat and then I pick her up, kicking the door closed behind me. I've had an idea. I place her down, so her arse is sat on the kitchen table and I head for the chocolate fountain, ripping the box open.

"What are you doing?" Kaylie asks. "I want you, not chocolate."

That's quite a statement given how much she loves chocolate.

"Why not have both?" I wink.

Thank goodness I once had to set up my mum's chocolate fountain, so I know what to do. Five minutes and it will all be done.

Five minutes for me to have my hands all over the woman watching me, wanting me. Her chest heaves with anticipation and need as she watches my every move.

"So, I'm going to take this dress off carefully because it looks expensive, but I'm keeping you in that pendant and earrings and the shoes."

"What about my undies?"

"Definitely coming off."

I lift her to her feet and turn her so her back is towards me and I undo the halter neck and let the material slide down to her feet, my lips littering kisses across the base of her back and shoulders, her skin pricking with goosebumps every time we connect. I pick her dress up and put it over the back of a chair. She's in front of me in lacy red panties and a lacy red bra and I could kick myself that it's taken me all these years to realise what I had in front of me all along. I place her back on the table and stand between her legs. Leaning down and kissing her, nipping at her mouth, her earlobe. Teasing kisses down her neck. Until the chocolate is ready.

Placing my finger in the bowl, I offer it to her lips. She takes my finger in, sucking greedily and my already hard cock strains painfully against my own trousers.

I take her hand and hold it against my dick. She wastes no time in unbuttoning my waistband and unzipping me, my trousers fall to my feet where I step out of them. I quickly take off my shirt, tie, shoes, and socks until I'm only in my boxers. Then I slip a breast out of Kaylie's bra and I coat it in chocolate before laving it off with my tongue. She whimpers, her head falling back and her back arching to offer more of herself to me. I repeat my actions with her other breast, ensuring I lick her clean of the sweet chocolate and then I kiss her. It's fucking heaven.

The chocolate plays its part as we feed each other spoonsful of melted chocolate and trail it down our bodies.

Eventually her need for me must get the better of her because she jumps down from the table and forces me to drop down onto one of her chairs.

She stands before me, her eyes slowly trailing down from my face and running over every line and indent of my chest and stomach. My cock visibly twitches behind the confines of my boxers. Noticing, her teeth sink into her bottom lip.

"Fuck, Kaylie." Her name is no more than a moan, my desire to feel her hands on my body too much.

Turning, she picks up a spoonful of the chocolate

and watches intently as it drips over my pecs and abs.

"I think this is going to be the best chocolate I've ever tasted."

I don't get a chance to respond because she leans forward and laps at my skin.

"Fuck." My hips thrust up at her contact. I need so much more from her.

She doesn't miss it. Looking up from under her lashes as she continues her trail down my body, excitement and hunger shines in their depths.

The moment she wraps her delicate fingers in the waistband of my boxers and pulls I almost come before I'm even free of the fabric.

Her eyes widen as she takes in my length but I don't miss the little smile of approval that twitches her lips.

I want to make a quip about my impressive pole, I usually would with any other woman. But this isn't any woman. This is Kaylie. *My woman.* That thought is only confirmed when she looks back up at me. The expression on her face is so serious and I breathe a sigh of relief that she feels exactly what I am right now.

This is it. This is everything she's been looking for.

Her small smile turns wicked and she pulls my boxers from my legs and drops to her knees before me, but not before she refills her spoon with chocolate.

The warm liquid is dribbled over my cock, my fists clenching around the wood beneath me as I try to keep control of myself.

I pride myself in being able to last as long as necessary. I don't want to embarrass myself before she's even fucking touched me.

All thoughts of my male ego vanish the second she hesitantly leans forward and licks at the chocolate that's about to drip from the end of my cock.

My grip damn near splinters the wood beneath me as I fight not to grasp her head and force her fully down onto my cock. My need to be fully seated in her hot mouth with her red lips wrapped around my width is almost too much to bear.

Those long minutes on that chair will go down (like she did) as one of the best moments of my entire life.

When I can't wait any longer. I fireman's lift her and carry her to her room before dropping her onto her brand new freshly made bed.

Climbing above her, I stare into her eyes. "If you

have any doubts, say so now and I promise I'll still be your best friend although my cock will not be."

"What a romantic sentiment." She eye-rolls. "Just fuck me already."

"Fuck. I don't have a condom."

"Top drawer." She meets my jealous gaze. "Just in case a miracle ever happened."

"Well women do shout 'Oh God' at me," I quip.

Condom rolled on, I line myself up next to her warm flesh and I slowly nudge against her, rolling my hips so I tease at her entrance.

She lifts her own hips up to try to get me nearer. I carry on teasing, just brushing the head of my cock near her heat. I capture her lips with mine and then I thrust in deep. She moans directly into my mouth with satisfaction. She still tastes of chocolate and I savour her flavours on my tongue.

I take my time, slowly pushing into her and teasing back out. She makes moans and mewls as I fuck her to the point where I'm on lust overload and I can't take it slow any more. I push to the hilt and quicken my pace, taking her along for the ride until she's shouting.

"Oh fuck. Aiden. I'm going to come. I'm..."

She explodes around me milking my own release and I collapse against her. Sweaty chocolately bodies combining. But I'm not satisfied. I need more and it's not chocolate on my tongue next as I lower myself between her legs and I bring her to another climax.

We snooze and fuck, snooze and... make love? We become slower, more intimate, and I find us staring into each other's eyes as we move together.

Finally exhausted, I spoon myself against her back and we fall asleep together.

SUNDAY MORNING DAWNS and I can't believe that when I wake up, I'm in bed with Kaylie and it feels right.

When she wakes, she turns around in my arms and looks up at me. Her expression says it all. She's wondering if it was alcohol talking and if I'm about to leave.

"When did this change?" she asks. "This thing between us. When did best friends become this?"

"For me it was when you went on the date and you didn't ring me. I was so used to being there for you. Being the one riding in on my white horse, well, okay in a white BMW; but I realised you were going to meet someone, and I realised I didn't like it. What about you?"

A blush hits her cheeks. "When we were in my single bed and you'd stayed over after the fire. I woke up with your cock digging in me. I wanted to rock back against it."

I grab her hips and pull her to me. "Like this?"

"Yeah, just like that." She rocks back against me and rubs against my dick. I slip myself between her legs and begin teasing her again with the head.

"You'd better get another condom out," she says suggestively.

"About that." I stop my motions and rest up on one elbow meeting her gaze directly on. "I'd not finished with my presents for you, and I was going to offer anyway, but now this has happened, well... if you want, we can make a baby together. You and me. We don't need to use condoms. Not if you don't want to."

Her eyes fill with tears and I'm inwardly congratulating myself on being Kaylie's hero, waiting for her to say, 'yes'.

"You absolute bastard." Comes from her mouth.

"What?"

She's out of bed in a flash, grabbing her robe and turning on me. "We have a shag and you offer to be my baby daddy? What was this then, a pity fuck? Oh let's get the sad old spinster drunk and laid on her birthday and then offer her a baby before her eggs die."

"What are you talking about?" I protest.

"I told you how I wanted to have a baby. You of all people know this. You know it more than anyone else. Candlelight, romance. The love of my life. That's my ideal. Having a donor is a means to an end, not my dream."

She's sobbing now, struggling to say the words.

"You made me feel like we were something. Something that might lead somewhere eventually. Maybe to that candlelight, but then you just basically offer me your sperm like the donor you are. Get out."

"You've got me all wrong, Kay-bear. Please listen to me."

"I said GET OUT. NOW. Before I ring Jenson and get him to throw you the fuck out. Leave me alone."

There's no talking to her, she's hysterical. I want to tell her I also want the candlelight and that I love her. That I can wait for kids or we can start right now. I want my forever with her.

I've fucked up. It's better I give her some time to calm down and then try to do damage control. Let the fire die down then secure it to stop it relighting remember?

"This is not over, Kaylie. We need to talk. But I'm giving you some time."

She won't even look me in the eye.

With my things gathered up, I leave her house and head towards the bus stop.

There should be a break glass for love emergencies.

I'd have shattered that fucker to pieces.

17

___

KAYLIE

IT'S BEEN a little over two weeks since I threw
Aiden out of my house.

A little over two weeks since I spoke to my best
friend. And although I've ignored all his calls, texts,
and visits, I miss him like crazy. Especially as I sit
on the edge of my bath waiting to find out our
fate.

It's been two days since I first suspected
something, but I just assumed that I was being
paranoid after having sex at last. But my period being
two days late is unheard of. Plus, there are the other
things that I've tried to blame on more obvious
things. I'm exhausted... it's just the end of term. I've
got this weird metallic taste in my mouth... I've just
run out of mouthwash. See, there are totally realistic

possibilities for everything, besides my missing period.

But how? I know we were drunk, but I remember each and every single time Aiden came inside me and I know full well that he had a condom on each time. I made sure of it after allowing my birth control to run out months ago seeing as I was getting precisely zero action.

My hands tremble as I stare at the white stick taunting me, face down on the basin. It's been over three minutes, I know it has, but I can't bring myself to do it.

I want a baby. I want one more than anything... well, that's not actually true. What I really want is a family. A mummy, a daddy, and a baby. And for a few hours two weeks ago I really started to think that Aiden could be it.

We both made the somewhat risky decision to act on how we'd been feeling and he gave me the best night of my life. Even now I get a little hot every time I see the fondue set. The way his tongue felt against my skin as he licked—no, stop it. This is not helping.

Shaking out my arms, I blow out a long breath and go for it.

"One... two... three..." I count out loud before turning it over.

Pregnant.

"Fuck."

I've no idea how I should feel in this moment. Part of me is ecstatic, another part disappointed, but mostly I'm just confused right now.

With the piss stick still in my hand, I make my way to my bedroom and drop down onto my new double bed.

Did he really think that I was such a sure thing that night that he even went to the liberty of buying a bed? Am I really that desperate and pathetic?

Trying to figure out where it all went wrong, I pull the top drawer of my bedside table open and pull out the box of condoms. It was full and now there's a lonely one left in the bottom. The knowledge of how many times we went at it that night colours my cheeks.

Turning the box over in my hand, my eyes almost pop out of my head.

"Fuck me, that can't be right."

Expires: 10 May 2017. They're over two years out of date.

Christ, my life is pathetic.

Seeing as school finished for the holidays on Friday, I drop the offending condom box along with the pee stick to the bedside table and I crawl back into bed in an attempt to avoid reality.

This cannot be happening to me.

I toss and turn for an hour or two before I eventually drift off into a fitful nap. I awake with a start as Aiden tells me he no longer wants anything to do with me after I admit that I'm pregnant with his child.

"It was a dream, it was a dream," I tell myself repeatedly as my heart races in fear.

I might not know what came over him to offer to give me a baby like he did. The whole thing was ludicrous seeing as we'd potentially just embarked on a relationship and it could have led there anyway. I know I probably should have dealt with the whole thing differently, but I freaked out. I'd just woken up a little worse for wear, naked with my best friend. My head was most definitely not in the right place for that kind of conversation, especially after having his fingers between my legs.

Dragging myself from my bed, I attempt to start my day again. Glancing at the clock, I realise I must have slept longer than I thought and I'm now running late. I'd promised I would meet Leah for a little last-minute Christmas shopping. She needs help with a few final things for my brother. I've already told her that I'll be no help because I struggle every year, but she was insistent. I'm assuming our little trip has more to do with me shutting myself off from the world, or more importantly Aiden, for the past two weeks.

I quickly get showered and dressed before grabbing my bag to leave the house. I check my phone and just like every morning since that day I find a morning message from Aiden begging me to talk to him.

At the beginning I received hourly messages and calls, but he's down to just a message twice a day now. It's starting to freak me out that he's moving on.

I need to talk to him. To try to explain myself. But now I'm even more scared than I was after the main event.

I meet Leah outside Selfridges. The second I'm in reaching distance, she opens her arms and pulls me into a hug. Her kindness is just what I need to push me over the edge and a sob rumbles up my throat.

"I'm so sorry," I say, taking a step back and wiping my tear-stained cheeks with the back of my hands.

"I think we need to go for coffee first, what do you say?"

I nod and mumble my agreement. Leah slips her arm through mine and she leads us towards the cafe.

"Cappuccino?" she asks once we're at the front of the queue.

"Ye—no! I'll have a hot chocolate. With cream and marshmallows," I quickly add. Leah looks at me curiously, but she keeps her mouth shut until we find ourselves a table.

"Talk," she demands. She might only be small but damn she's a force to be reckoned with. No wonder my brother didn't stand a chance.

"I'm... I'm pregnant." The words feel alien passing my lips. It's something I've dreamt of being able to say for so long, but this was not at all how I planned it.

"You got a secret boyfriend we don't know about?"

"It was Aiden," I whisper it so quietly that she's no chance of hearing over the hustle and bustle going on around us.

"It's who?" she asks, her brows drawn together as she leans in to be able to hear better.

"It's Aiden's."

"Shut the fucking front door! It's Aiden's," she squeals so loudly that I wouldn't be surprised if the entire population of Selfridges didn't hear her.

Dropping my head into my hands I groan out my frustration with this whole situation.

"Oh my god. You and Aiden slept together at last."

"What do you mean 'at last'?"

"Oh come off it. The sexual tension between you two was so fucking obvious to everyone besides the two of you. I don't know how you couldn't see it at your birthday, he was practically drooling every time he so much as glanced in your direction."

"It happened on my birthday."

"OMG, was it amazing? Was he amazing?"

"Not really the most pressing issue right now."

"Humour me."

"It was incredible, but I didn't realise at the time that the condoms I have were from the Jurassic period."

Leah winces although the smile never leaves her face. "Maybe it was meant to happen."

"What's that supposed to mean?"

"Oh come on. You and Aiden are meant to be. You should have been a couple from the get go. This is just the universe's way of forcing your hands."

"He has no idea."

"I assumed that seeing as you're still refusing to talk to him. He's been to the house and everything to try to get our help. He's a mess, Kay. You need to contact him."

"What if he hates me and thinks I did this to trap him?" I don't mention his suggestion of being my sperm donor so my argument might be a moot point if he really was willing to help me.

"This is Aiden we're talking about. He's so in love with you. He's about to dive headfirst into self-destruction mode if he doesn't hear from you soon, so you need to pull up your big girl panties and get your arse over to his house. He needs rescuing from himself."

Leah's words ring through my ears throughout our entire shopping trip.

Aiden needs rescuing.

I blame it on the pregnancy hormones raging inside my body but before heading home, I stop at a fancy-dress shop and pick up something that's a sure-fire way to get his attention. He's spent almost his entire life rescuing me from my own disastrous mistakes. It's time for me to don the uniform and do a little lifesaving of my own.

It's as I'm outside my house that I hear a voice I never wanted to hear again. I turn and face Phillip.

"You've got some nerv—"

"Will you just hear me out? Please. I'm sorry,

about the fire. I didn't know they'd fallen from my pocket..."

"Save it. I'm not interested in your apology. Where was it when I was in hospital, hey?"

"I didn't think I'd get anywhere near you. Not with *him* there. I knew he looked familiar. Bloody Aiden. Coming to the rescue. What a hero."

"Phillip." I shout it this time. "Go home. I'm not interested in anything you have to say."

"But I came back here for you. We're both single; we used to be good together. We can be again. And my parents ask about you all the time. They were never happy I left you. Told me I'd made a mistake and I agree with them. They're threatening to cut me out of my inheritance if I don't settle down soon."

There it is. The truth about why he came back. He's not interested in me, just in money.

"Listen to me. We were over the minute you left and as you moved on with your life, I also moved on with mine. I don't love you. To be truthful, I don't even like you. Your actions almost meant the death of myself and five children and you turn up here without so much as a bunch of flowers. Your apology is about as genuine as the fake Rolex on your wrist. Now I'm busy and you're in my way so kindly fuck off."

"Well, I don't think—"

"I don't care what you fucking think, that's my whole point. Goodbye, Phillip." I walk away, into the main building of the flats and I feel good to finally have spoken my truth to my ex. Now with the past dealt with, it was time to face my future.

I strip out of my clothes the second I walk in through the front door. I hit the shower and shave, scrub, and buff my entire body in the hope of not being sent away with my tail between my legs later.

I pull on my new outfit and laugh at myself when I look in the mirror. He'd better find this amusing because I look like an idiot.

I curl my hair and do my make up just like I did for my birthday. I remember all too well how his eyes widened when he saw me that evening and I'd really love a repeat of that.

My hands tremble as I gather up my stuff to leave the house. If I weren't in my current condition I might down a shot or two before going out in public like this, but that's not an option; not for the next few months anyway.

When I pull the main door to the building open, my taxi is idling outside. I might feel ridiculous but I'm not stupid enough to go out like this on public transport.

"Where to, love?"

I reel off Aiden's address like I have a million times before, but I've never felt so nervous before that I might puke.

When we pull up outside his home, I fear I might hyperventilate with how fast my heart's pounding.

"Thank you." I pay for my short journey and hop out of his car.

My knees are weak as I make my way up the driveway to his house.

After giving myself a talking to, I lift my hand and knock on his front door.

Everything's silent and I start to think he's not here. He's probably at work. My level of stupidity starts to get the better of me and I'm just about to slink away like this never happened when I hear movement behind the door.

My heart thunders and my hands tremble as I wait for the door to open, but when it does, it doesn't reveal the man I need to see.

"Brandon," I breathe, disappointment threatening to break me.

"Wow, girl. You're looking smokin'. Aiden will be gutted he missed this. You got some kinky Christmas party to attend?"

"Something like that," I mutter, my cheeks burning red. "Where is he?"

"He's out with some woman."

"Aiden's on a... date?" The words feel wrong even coming out of my mouth.

"Yeah. How don't you know about her? I thought you two shared everything beside saliva."

I screw up my nose at his assumption. Although we all know he's wrong.

"Do you know where he's meeting her?"

He gives me the name of the restaurant and I just about manage to contain my smile as I discover he's at my usual date restaurant.

Is it a sign?

"Thanks, you've been so helpful."

Brandon nods and goes back into hiding. I've no idea if he has any intention of finding himself a woman or not but if he does, then he really needs to have a good look in the mirror because he looks like a hobo on his best days.

I call for another taxi as I descend the stairs and plan out my mission.

18

AIDEN

IT'S BEEN TWO WEEKS.

Two miserable weeks.

I've been such an arse pain at work that Jess, one of our female firefighters insisted that I come out with her tonight. She said it was just as mates, that I remind her of her younger brother, and he ended up seeing a psychiatrist after the end of a relationship. I seriously hope she doesn't try to hit on me though.

"Tell me about her then." Jess tilts her head, her bright red fringe falling in her eyes. She bats it away.

"Who?"

"The woman who finally broke Mr Sexy Fireman. We've been waiting all these years, you know? Watching you flirt with all these women, breaking hearts wherever you go, and we've all wanted to see the moment you fell. So who is it?"

"Doesn't matter. She doesn't want me."

Jess orders me another beer while we wait for our table to be ready. She makes out she's being generous, but I know she wants to loosen my tongue. I've used that trick many a time to loosen a woman's inhibitions. No, I'm not proud, but I was a manwhore, we've established that.

"Who is it? Is it... Kaylie?"

"What? How do you...? Has she been talking to you?" That's not possible, they've never met.

"Aiden. All the watch know you're in love with your best friend. That's why we think you've never settled down, just distracted yourself with other women, none of them ever measuring up."

Did everyone in the universe know I had the hots for Kaylie? Seems they all knew before I did.

I slump, taking a big slug of my pint. "She doesn't want me."

"No?"

"No. We slept together, and I messed up, and now she won't even speak to me."

"Hmmm. Does Kaylie have light-brown, curly hair? Is she tall and slim, but has amazing legs?"

"Erm, yeah." My mouth salivates thinking about her thighs and what's between them.

"See you at work, bro." Jess jumps off her barstool and I turn around to see what the fuck she's playing at and then I don't even care, because Kaylie is walking towards me dressed as the hottest female firefighter I've ever seen. She's a walking wet dream.

I jump down and run towards her, sweeping her up in the air. She shrieks, so I lower her back down, sliding her against my body as I do so.

"What are you doing here?"

"I'm rescuing you from yourself. You shouldn't be dating other women. Not when you're mine."

"It wasn't a date. She's a colleague, but you got one thing right. I'm yours." My mouth claims hers and I hear whoops and hollers from other people in the restaurant, mainly from the staff who've been rooting for us from the get-go.

Eventually we part and I grab her hand and bid goodnight to everyone. "We're going to mine. Brandon will be at work now," I tell her.

There's a reason I chose mine that becomes apparent as Kaylie sits in the living room where I've asked her to wait.

"Okay." I tell her. "Let's go."

I walk towards my bedroom with her and when

she pushes open the door, she sees it. There are about fifty candles around the room, all lit, all giving the room a flickering glow. "This isn't for conceiving children," I tell her. "This is for every night. I will always give you candlelight and romance if you want it, Kaylie Hale. I love you."

Her eyes swim with tears as she looks around. "I love you too."

That's all I needed to hear. I carefully lift and place her on the bed and then I strip us both naked and kiss her for what feels like forever.

I'm so desperate to be inside her. My fingers tease her wet heat until I know she's on the brink and then I lean over to grab a condom. She grabs my wrist and shakes her head. "You don't have to do that."

"Really?" I feel my own eyes moisten. Fuck, is this really happening? "Kaylie Hale, I hope we make a baby, and I hope you know I intend to make you happy for the rest of your life."

I push inside her and her legs wrap around mine. As my climax fills her with everything I have, I realise that I'm exactly where I want to be.

Nestled in my arms she says, "I'm pregnant."

I laugh. "I know I'm good but even I'm not that fast."

She turns so she's looking up at me with those big

doe-eyes. "No, Aid. The condoms in my drawer. Erm, they were really old." Her cheeks colour. "They didn't work. That night. You, erm, made me pregnant."

My eyes widen and my hand trails across her stomach. "Are you serious? Our baby is in there?"

She nods her head.

I move down her body and I kiss the soft flesh of her stomach.

"Well, hey there, baby. I'm your daddy, and I'm going to be the best daddy ever. But while you're cooking in there can you cover your ears because I'm about to do things to your mummy right now that you shouldn't be witness to."

I move further down the bed until my mouth is between Kaylie's legs. Kaylie's satisfaction is my target now and forever. My fireman's hose for one girl, and her only.

I'm going to be a dad.

We're going to be parents.

Kaylie Hale is mine.

She doesn't know it yet, but I intend to move into her place and we'll make it ours. At Christmas there'll be a massive sparkling tree, but the best gift won't be under it.

It'll be the girl right next to me and the gift waiting to be unwrapped in her tummy.

I can't wait.

EPILOGUE

Nine months later
August

Aiden

KAYLIE, and our two-day-old son, Josh, are home from the hospital. I can't stop smiling. I watch from the doorway as Kaylie introduces our son to his new partner in crime, Jenson and Leah's son, Albie, who was born two months before.

Jenson walks over and smiles.

"We did good."

"We did."

We look over at our women and babies. Amelia is demanding to have a turn in holding Josh.

"Daddy." Amelia looks up at Jenson. "You said babies came from mummy's tummies, but Alex in my class says they come from pussies. You need to tell him that that's kittens. He's confused."

I guffaw with laughter. Amelia joins in.

"I know, right, Uncle Aiden? As if babies come from pussies."

Tears are streaming down my cheeks.

"You can laugh. You have all this to come." Jenson raises a brow.

"Can't wait, mate. I've never been so happy." My eyes meet Kaylie's and I see everything I feel reflected right back.

When they've left and Josh is sleeping soundly in his crib, I slip up into our bedroom and grab what I need. My heart is thudding in my chest and I think I might actually pass out.

Walking back into the living room, I sit on the sofa next to Kaylie and I grab her hand.

"Thank you, Kaylie Hale, for our son. He is the most beautiful baby I've ever seen."

She smiles, a big beaming smile. "Yeah, he really is."

"Now." I swallow. "Forgive me for snooping around in your things, but I've been on the hunt for a piece of paper I knew you wrote when you were fifteen. I didn't have to look far. By the way, is that all new underwear ready for after the six-week-check?" I wink.

Kaylie's eyes have widened. "Never mind about that. What about my piece of paper?"

I take it from my pocket and read.

"Kaylie Hale's ideal proposal and wedding. I don't care how the love of my life proposes as long as it's romantic and memorable, but I want a huge wedding, with the most gorgeous dress, bridesmaids, pageboys, and flowers and candles everywhere. I'd love a huge diamond ring with one great big square stone and two smaller stones next to it on an 18-carat-gold thick band."

Kaylie is visibly shaking in front of me. I take her by the hand and picking up our sleeping son, I make her follow me out of the building. As we approach the communal garden she gasps, as Jenson steps forward to take hold of Josh.

Our family and friends are gathered in the garden, which is decorated in bunting with the words WILL YOU MARRY ME? draped between the trees.

Taking the ring out of my pocket, I drop to my knees.

"So, Kaylie Hale. Will you be my wife?"

"Yes." Tears are rolling down her cheeks as I place the ring, the one exactly as she described, on her finger. "Oh my god, yes."

Everyone cheers as I kiss my new fiancée. "You can arrange whatever wedding you want. Just tell me what I need to do, what you want, and it's yours. I love you, Kaylie."

She scrunches up the note and puts it in her pocket. "I have everything I need. As long as I become Mrs Kaylie Thomson, I don't care how we do it."

We kiss to more whoops and cheers as she whispers in my ear.

"And yes, that underwear is for in a few week's time."

My fiancée stokes a fire in me that I don't want rescuing from.

THE END

Until... BRANDON is back in THE DADDY DILEMMA.

DOWNLOAD NOW

Read on for a sneak peek...

SNEAK PEEK
THE DADDY DILEMMA

Brandon

December

"This is an intervention, mate."

The voice of my best mate, Jack, booms from about a foot away from me. Am I still asleep? Is this a dream Jack or a real Jack?

I realise it's a real Jack as I roll onto my back, a corner of something digging in my thigh painfully as I do so. Rubbing at my eyes, I sit up and squint. The bastard's opened the curtains and winter sunshine lasers through my vision. I bet I have empty sockets now. Eyeballs disintegrated. What the fuck is digging in my leg? I reach down and unearth a pizza box from underneath me. I'm still wearing my uniform from LoCost, the bargain warehouse I work nights at as a manager. I feel hot and sweaty despite it being winter. Oh, that might be because I turned the thermostat up on my way in last night. I don't think I'll want to open my heating bill.

"You awake yet?"

I nod though I'm not sure it's the truth. I watch as Aiden, my ex-housemate walks into the room. Ah, now I see how Jack got in.

"Wassgoinnonn?" I mumble.

"What's going on, my friend, is that we're taking you in hand. Enough is enough. You've been slobbing around for long enough and since Aiden left you've got a whole lot worse. I get married in a week's time. A week. You will not spoil my bride's Christmas Eve wedding by turning up looking like a hobo. We're Queer Eye-ing you.

That wakes me up. What the hell is that?

I stare at him wide-eyed. "What does that mean? It sounds sexual. Anything weird should be happening to you at your stag do." I startle as a thought comes to me. "Oh shit, is that tonight?"

"Yes, it's tonight. It's in... let me see." Jack looks at his watch. "Five hours time. Five hours to do something with you. Now Queer Eye, you muppet, is a Netflix show where five gay guys make people over. Clothes, hair, cooking skills, house, and life."

Now I'm starting to feel very worried about where this is headed. I think my head is where it's headed.

Aiden pipes up. "You're needing someone to share with to pay half the rent when my notice period is paid up. I paid you until the end of January because moving out at Christmas sucks, I know, but you need to get yourself and this house in order." He looks around the place taking in discarded beer cans, takeaway cartons, and is that an actual pair of my briefs? "No one is going to move in *here*." He says the word like most people say the word Brexit, i.e. with high disdain and as if it's the worst subject in the whole world.

He hands me a coffee, one I thought he'd made for himself. Mmmm, he's made it just as I like it. I miss Aiden making me coffee and it's only been a couple of weeks since he moved out. He fell in love. Can't blame him. Kaylie is lovely. I knew he wanted her before he did, the idiot. "How's Kaylie?" I ask, taking a sip of the hot beverage.

"We're not here to talk about Kaylie. We are here for you and the clock is ticking. Get that down your neck, go get the quickest shower in history, and then we're off to the centre of London, my friend, where you are booked to have your hair restyled, and we doing some clothes shopping. Oh and I saw your bank statement, so I know you've been saving your earnings since the end of time and have more than enough for some new threads. We're buying you a whole new wardrobe including clothes for tonight. And I've also organised someone to come around later in the week to help you sort through this mess of a house. When New Year is out of the way, you get this place advertised, you hear? And you keep it tidy. We'll be watching you."

Aiden points two fingers at his eyes, then at me and then back at himself.

My mouth has fallen open. In all the time I house-shared with Aiden he moaned at me plenty but then usually had a mad tidy up himself and just threw my shit in my room. But now he seems so... fierce.

"But I like my hair," I protest, holding onto my shoulder-length locks.

"Nope. Goodbye to lanky locks, goodbye to the bird's nest you have going on around your chin." Jack has his hands folded across his chest in a 'brook no argument' stance. "Do what you like after the wedding, but you're looking shipshape for my big day."

"I fully intended to shower for it."

"Nope, Reese is right. You need a tidy up."

I might have known she'd be behind all this. I've not seen her since the engagement party. I'll tolerate her at the wedding and then at the reception I'll make sure I'm at the opposite end of the room. If she comes over passing judgement on me, I might just be tempted to stick the bride's bouquet where the sun doesn't shine. God, what is it about her? I'm the most easy-going person I know but she brings out my inner twat.

My drink is taken out of my hand and I'm dragged off the sofa and pushed in the direction of the shower. My God, what is actually happening in my life right now? And do I have any clean towels?

DOWNLOAD NOW

ALSO BY ANGEL & TRACY

HOT SINGLE DAD ROMANCE

BAD INC BILLIONAIRES

ABOUT ANGEL DEVLIN

Angel Devlin writes stories as hot as her coffee. She lives in Sheffield with her partner, son, and a gorgeous whippet called Bella.

Newsletter:
Sign up here for Angel's latest news and exclusive content.
https://geni.us/angeldevlinnewsletter

ABOUT TRACY LORRAINE

Tracy Lorraine is a new adult and contemporary romance author. Tracy is in her thirties and lives in a cute Cotswold village in England with her husband and daughter. Having always been a bookaholic with her head stuck in her Kindle, Tracy decided to try her hand at a story idea she dreamt up and hasn't looked back since.

Be the first to find out about new releases and offers. Sign up to my newsletter here.

If you want to know what I'm up to and see teasers and snippets of what I'm working on, then you need to be in my Facebook group. Join Tracy's Angels here.

Keep up to date with Tracy's books at
www.tracylorraine.com

Printed in Great Britain
by Amazon

42952340R00118